OLIVER TRUSLER

I Must Get Back To The Woods

Copyright © 2023 by Oliver Trusler

All rights reserved. No part of this publication may be reproduced, stored or transmitted in any form or by any means, electronic, mechanical, photocopying, recording, scanning, or otherwise without written permission from the publisher. It is illegal to copy this book, post it to a website, or distribute it by any other means without permission.

This novel is entirely a work of fiction. The names, characters and incidents portrayed in it are the work of the author's imagination. Any resemblance to actual persons, living or dead, events or localities is entirely coincidental.

Oliver Trusler asserts the moral right to be identified as the author of this work.

Oliver Trusler has no responsibility for the persistence or accuracy of URLs for external or third-party Internet Websites referred to in this publication and does not guarantee that any content on such Websites is, or will remain, accurate or appropriate.

Designations used by companies to distinguish their products are often claimed as trademarks. All brand names and product names used in this book and on its cover are trade names, service marks, trademarks and registered trademarks of their respective owners. The publishers and the book are not associated with any product or vendor mentioned in this book. None of the companies referenced within the book have endorsed the book.

First edition

*This book was professionally typeset on Reedsy.
Find out more at reedsy.com*

In memory of Mark Linkous
I hope you finally made it back to the woods

Contents

1	1
2	3
3	6
4	8
5	12
6	14
7	16
8	18
9	23
10	25
11	27
12	29
13	34
14	36
15	39
16	43
17	45
18	51
19	53
20	57
21	59
22	62
23	66
24	70
25	79
26	81

27	85
28	89
29	91
30	97
31	100
32	103
33	105
34	109
35	112
36	115
37	120
38	123
39	126
40	128
41	133
42	141
43	145
44	150
45	154
46	161
47	164
48	167
49	172
50	177
51	182
52	185
53	194
54	198
55	202
56	208
About the Author	209

1

Goddammit! This is the third time this year I have woken up missing a hand.

Not to mention the mother of all hangovers, what did I even do last night and how much did I drink?

I need to retrace my steps, figure out where that hand has gone, first I need to be caffeinated.

It's surprising how difficult a simple task like making coffee becomes when you only have one hand, it's the sort of thing that doesn't feel like a two hand job until you actually try it. I guess you'd get used to it eventually but it's not like I always only have one hand and I don't intend on staying this way for long enough to become accustomed to it.

Perhaps I should explain to clear up some confusion.

My name is Jackson Bartholomew Harris (yeah, I know) everyone but my mum just calls me Jack, I'm 27 years old; Oh and I was born with the ability to detach and reattach my limbs at will, that bits quite important at this point.

Sounds fun right? But this is no superhero origin story, being able to detach your limbs is a largely useless superpower. It's a party trick, nothing more.

How does it work? Well I don't really know. All I know is I can separate my limbs at various points, wrists, elbows, shoulders, ankles, knees and hips. There's no blood, the remaining body is simply skin, as if the missing part was never there.

They don't pop off randomly; I have to think about doing it as well as the physical act of removing the body part. To reattach I simply hold the part in place and, for want of a better word, 'will' it together.

As I say, fairly useless, I mean when has having less body parts than the average human ever been a plus?

So, back to the matter at hand, I have woken up with my left hand missing at the wrist, a pounding headache and an almost irresistible urge to throw up. A couple of paracetamol and the coffee was helping with the hangover, now I need to find that hand.

2

After racking my brain for sometime it became abundantly clear I could remember bugger all about last night, I was going to need some help.

I sent a text to the only person who I could guarantee would have been with me on a night out, my best friend Alex.

You up?

I went to put the kettle on for another coffee, as expected a good ten minutes passed before I received a reply.

Think I'm dead

I'm coming over, put some clothes on

k

I grabbed my wallet and keys, struggled into a hoodie and left the flat.

My car was still in its usual parking spot on the street so seemed clear I must have gone out without it last night, otherwise I would have left it either at Alex's or the pub.

I drive an automatic (for obvious reasons) but it's still a pain getting it into drive with no left hand. My stump however works surprisingly well for jabbing the indicator. As I pulled up to Alex's house a few minutes later I saw him standing on the front porch vaping, as I approached I identified the smell of tobacco and candy floss, a distinctly unpleasant combination. He was wearing boxer shorts and a t-shirt that appeared to be more curry than cotton; his various mismatched tattoos were on show. He was always asking me when I was going to get one but I found it hard to commit to a t-shirt let alone permanent inking.

"I said to put some clothes on" I said

"I did, you should have seen me before"

"Glad I missed that, I need your help"

"Lost a hand again?"

"Yep."

"Third time this year?"

"Yep."

Alex's house was large but shared between 3 other people, 2 of which I knew pretty well, the third I had never seen. We went into the shared kitchen, the room was a horrible orange colour and every available surface appeared to be covered with stuff, plates, bowls, boxes of pasta, tins of food etc., one of his housemates, Susan, was at the table eating cereal.

"Morning Jack, good night last night?" She asked.

"Morning Suzy, I have no idea. Which usually means it was a good night I guess".

"Typical of you two, I see you are missing a hand again, what did you do with it this time?"

"I wish I knew, I'm hoping Alex will use his genius retracing skills to help me find it".

Behind me Alex snorted, Susan ignored him.

"Can't you wiggle it and walk it home like the hand in the Addams Family?"

"It doesn't work like that, once detached it's totally separate from me, I do get a sort of 'phantom limb' feeling but I have no control over it."

"Well that's shit. Anyway I've got work, good luck" Susan put her bowl in the sink on top of an ever increasing pile of used bowls, plates and cups and went into her room on the ground floor which would have been the living room if they hadn't turned every available space into a bedroom to make the rent cheaper.

Alex handed me a cup of coffee, the cup looked like it hadn't been cleaned since Thatcher was in power, I took it but didn't dare drink from it.

Alex sat down and said "What's the plan then?"

"I'm hoping you can help, I have no idea where we went last night"

Alex thought for a minute then said "Nope, I'm drawing a blank too, although...."

"Although what?"

"I'm pretty sure we started at the Duck and Goose"

"We always start at the Duck and Goose, did we stay there all night?".

"No idea mate but it's all I've got at the moment, it's far too early to be thinking; but if we go there it might jog my memory".

I sighed "Fine, let's head there and see what happens, can you drive though?" I waved my stump at him.

"Of course dude, I'll put some trousers on".

3

When I was a toddler, according to my parents, I used to like to stick anything I could get my hands on into my mouth. Lego bricks, TV remotes, discarded socks and all manner of items. My mum was constantly grabbing things out of my hands as I gleefully tried to shove said item into my gaping gob, it's a miracle I never choked really.

On one occasion my parents were watching TV and I was sat on the floor playing with my toys, my mum realized I was sucking on something so she wearily came over to stop me doing it. She got the shock of her life when she saw me sucking on my right foot, it no longer being attached to my right leg.

There was a lot of screaming and crying before my parents realized I wasn't injured and seemed quite content. Nevertheless they rushed me to A&E, the detached foot carried in a plastic Sainsbury's bag, to the nurse on the front desk they said I had an injury on my leg and needed to see a doctor urgently. It was not something they could explain and didn't want to mention that their child's foot had fallen off in the middle of a crowded hospital.

The doctor who saw me was baffled as you would expect. I had no injury to my leg; it looked and felt like I had been born without a right foot. The foot itself appeared undamaged and a perfect example of a young child's foot…just not attached to any leg. In desperation he held the foot up to the stump of my leg, perhaps to see if it had actually come from me or was some elaborate prank my parents played on unsuspecting doctors.

The foot of course magically reattached itself to my leg and I gleefully giggled and wiggled my toes, the doctor, in my parents words, went ghostly white and looked like he was about to pass out.

After gently tugging on my feet and finding they remained firmly in place the three of them discussed what had happened and it was agreed that they would not mention the phenomenon to anyone, deciding that no one would believe them and without any proof it would make the doctor look like a fool.

We were sent home, the incident not being recorded on my medical record and a promise that it would not be mentioned to anyone. The doctor gave my parents his personal phone number and address and requested that if anything like this happened again they should immediately contact him. I guess he felt this could be a chance at becoming famous if he could prove it happened, if not he did not want to look like a lunatic in front of his peers.

The incident was never mentioned again and some years passed without anything untoward occurring to my feet or any other appendages. By all accounts I was a perfectly normal child.

That is until I turned 11 years old.

4

The Duck and Goose was your normal town pub, the exterior was an old building that had probably stood for hundreds of years and once upon a time it was probably used for something more important then downing pints. It was also closed and wouldn't open for another hour, this didn't stop Alex from banging on the door and shouting for the landlord.

"TOM! TOM!" Alex yelled.

"I'm pretty sure his name is Bill." I said

"Really? Damn, I always called him Tom"

"Yeah and he has corrected you so many times I think he has given up and accepted his new life as Tom".

Alex banged on the door a few more times then said

"Well whatever his name is he's not answering, let's go round the back".

"How would that help" I replied.

"I dunno, might jog my memory, the smoking area is round the back and I probably vaped a lot last night"

"You know you can vape inside right?"

"Yeah but I miss the experience of smoking, standing in the wet and the cold, aah memories"

"Weirdo"

The two of us walked around to the back of the pub where a small patio area with a couple of tables and chairs stood empty, the double doors leading into the bar were locked tight, you could see the tatty red chairs had been turned upside down and put on top of the tables, the lights that surrounded the bar were all out but it was clear no one was inside.

Alex rattled them aggressively just to double check.

Just then a bundle of ginger fur shot out from under a bin and ran across the patio and under the door of a shed.

"Did you see that?" I asked

"See what?" Alex turned from the doors he was peering into.

"Something just ran out from those bins and into that shed, I think it was a cat"

"So?"

"Well, I'm pretty sure it had six legs". I said, still not quite believing it myself.

"Six legs? You sure? Are you high?"

"Pretty sure, and no, not right now, a little hung over maybe but I'm not hallucinating".

"Well then this requires further investigation" Alex said as he walked over to the shed.

The shed looked old but sturdy, nothing special about it, roughly the size of a phone box, if you can remember what those looked like. The odd thing was the shiny industrial sized padlock keeping the door locked; it seemed overkill for a standard shed.

"I'll pick the lock!" Alex said pulling out a hair clip and jamming it into the keyhole.

"Since when could you pick locks?" I asked

"Since I saw a YouTube video on it last week, it looks easy enough."

I was not convinced but let him get on with it whilst I inspected the door further, then I noticed it.

"Alex." I said.

"One second nearly got it."

"Alex!"

"What?" He looked up at me.

"The padlock isn't doing anything".

"It will if you let me concentrate".

"No I mean it's on wrong, someone put it on the wrong way, the latch can be opened."

Alex looked doubtful but turned back to the lock and easily slid the latch to one side.

"Huh, how about that."

Slowly, Alex pulled the door open and we both stared inside.

The interior of the shed opened out into a dark metal tunnel which ran far deeper than the outside of the shed would allow, Alex and I looked at each other and then both went to the back of the shed.

It was solid and nothing behind it, we went back to the front, I cautiously touched the metal walls of the tunnel, they were oddly warm to the touch, not hot but a comforting natural warmth.

"Put your phone light on" I instructed Alex

"Oh I'm gonna film this!" Alex took out his phone and started recording with the flash on.

The flash lit up the beginning of the tunnel, about ten feet in the ginger cat sat staring back at us shocked at the sudden light, it clearly had six legs, three on each side, apart from this abnormality the cat looked like any other cat.

"Shit!" Said the cat and disappeared into the darkness.

"What the hell?" I said looking at Alex.

"I heard it too, and that is definitely a six legged cat, a six legged talking cat! We're going to be rich YouTube stars with this!" He was clearly more excited than shocked.

"Let's follow it" He said and stepped into the shed.

"Is that really a good idea? This is getting too weird for me"

"It can never get too weird my friend, let's just see if we can get another shot of the cat" He walked further into the shed his camera light illuminating the tunnel which appeared to be lined with metal plates on all sides, floor and roof included.

I hesitantly followed him; the tunnel seemed to go on forever with no change for some time until we saw something lying on the metal floor in the distance.

"What's that?" I whispered.

"Not sure, let's have a look" Alex whispered back. I have no idea why we were whispering but it seemed appropriate.

As we got nearer Alex hissed "I think it's a hand! Is it yours?"

"I would assume so, unless there are multiple missing hands in the area, go grab it so I can reattach it".

Alex crouched down as he approached the hand, just as he reached for it the cat appeared from the darkness, grabbed the hand in his mouth and shot back away.

"Shit!" Said Alex, "Sneaky bastard!"

"Quick get after him, I need that hand back!" We started to run down the tunnel, as we did it appeared to be getting lighter. And lighter.

Soon it was so bright we were practically blinded as lightness flooded the metal tunnel.

"Jesus, what's happening?" I yelled to Alex closing my eyes to shield the light.

"I have no idea" As he spoke the light grew to a seemingly impossible intensity and then my world went black.

5

The next thing I knew I was back in my bed alone in the flat; I was in my underwear and still missing my left hand. What had happened? How did I get back here?

I scanned around for my phone and there it was on my side table plugged in same as I always leave it when I go to bed, I picked it up and immediately text Alex.

What the hell?

I threw some clothes on and grabbing my keys rushed out the door.

My car was in its usual place which made no sense as it should have been at Alex's house where I left it. As I climbed in my phone buzzed, it was Alex replying.

Eh? A helpful reply.

On my way over I text back, shoving the phone in my pocket I sped out of the road and headed to Alex's house.

Alex again greeted me at the door; he was wearing the same clothes as before, vaping the same noxious combination.

"What's up with you?" He asked.

"What happened yesterday?" I asked

Alex laughed "Yeah I don't remember much either, I see you lost your hand again. Must have been a good night!"

"What? No I mean with the talking cat and the tunnel in the shed."

"Um, OK. Did you maybe take something last night and are still feeling the effects?"

Alex had no idea what I was talking about, I don't know if he was going mad or I was, then I remembered something.

"Get your phone" I said and followed Alex into the house; he grabbed his phone from his room and met me in the kitchen.

Suzy was sat eating cereal again, just like yesterday.

"What are you two up to?" She asked whilst crunching away.

"Jack thinks we met a talking cat in a tunnel last night or something" Alex said handing me his phone.

"Here I'll show you." I opened the video folder on Alex's phone and opened the newest one. Holding it out so Alex and Suzy could both see as well I hit play.

The video showed the dark metal tunnel, it was shaky from being held while walking down the tunnel.

"See?" I said

"I don't remember this" said Alex "Where's this cat?"

"Just wait!"

The video continued down the tunnel and then a flash of light and it just stopped.

"Well that was weird" Suzy returned to eating her breakfast.

"No there was more, there was a cat! It had six legs and it stole my hand!" I started the video again and re-watched it, nothing changed. There was no sign of a cat or my hand.

Alex and Suzy looked at each other.

"I don't get it" I slumped into a chair.

"Me neither, when did we go into a tunnel?" Alex asked

"Yesterday morning, when we went to the pub to look for my hand, is none of this ringing a bell?"

Alex thought for a minute then replied:

"Yesterday was Friday, I was at work in the morning, we didn't go to the pub till the evening."

"No yesterday was Saturday....wasn't it?" I was unsure of anything now.

Suzy tapped at the top of the phone screen which clearly displayed the date, it was indeed Saturday morning. Somehow I had gone back a day.

"This is fucked up!" I said.

6

On my eleventh birthday my parents threw me a party, all my friends from school were invited along with their parents, balloons and banners were hung, a huge chocolate cake shaped like a hedgehog was sitting ready for me to blow the candles out when the time came.

Early afternoon the guests began to arrive, the presents were piling up and I was getting giddy and restless wanting to open them all but my parents insisted I greet everyone at the door wearing my, as they called it, adorable suit. I was required to shake the hands of each and every parent who arrived.

Of course I just wanted to eat food, play with my friends and unwrap all the gifts that had been brought for me. "Just the Williams to come then you can go play" my mum said, making me excited that the dull part of the day was nearly over.

Mr and Mrs. Williams arrived shortly and I was jumping from foot to foot in anticipation of going back to play with the friends who had already arrived. I greeted Stephen, the Williams son who although attended the same school as me we weren't really friends, parents have a habit of thinking all kids the same age must be friends. When it came to shake the hands of the parents I dutifully shook Mr. Williams hand then rushed to shake his wife's hand, in my excitement I had already turned to run back into the house before I'd finished shaking her hand.

It was as I ran I heard a shriek behind me and turned to see Mrs. Williams holding what appeared to be a human hand. I looked down at my own arm and realized the hand was mine. It was my turn to shriek and I cried out for my mother who grabbed the hand from the startled guest, scooped me up and ran into the bedroom with me.

My dad apologized to all the guests and informed them I had been playing a prank and somehow injured myself. He made excuses and asked everyone to leave so they could take me to see a doctor.

My parents sat down with me and after calming each other down they held the small hand up to my wrist, of course it reattached and my crying stopped immediately, my fear turning to curiosity. I wiggled my fingers and asked if I could now open my presents.

Whilst I joyfully unwrapped toys and games, piling up the wrapping paper in the corner of the living room my father called the doctor we had seen several years earlier. Surprisingly the number still worked and he agreed to meet with us the following day.

The doctor came to our house and sat with me patiently asking me question after question; he would gently tug on my hand or foot and ask if it felt loose or different in any way. I said no, it feels like it always feels. He was frustrated and I was bored, at this point I somehow decided what I should to and the next time he tugged on my hand I let it come off. He yelled, part in surprise and part in glee, I laughed thinking it the most hilarious thing I had ever seen.

After detaching and reattaching my hand several times the doctor announced he knew of a special facility that would be able to examine me fully and diagnose what was happening. By this point my parents were flabbergasted and agreed to take me to the facility.

Within a week I had been taken out of school and arrived at the shady looking building on the outskirts of London where I would end up living for some time.

I never saw those friends who attended my party again. The Williams apparently moved away not long after the incident.

7

I was sat on Alex's bed holding a cup of lukewarm tea (I had insisted on a clean, well *cleaner*, mug than the one I had been given yesterday, today, this morning? Who even knew any more).

Alex's room was exactly what you would expect a student's room to be, piles of clothes everywhere, empty beer bottles scattered around, dirty cups and plates littering the room, a filthy looking bong stood on the bedside table. The walls were lined with posters from various movies and bands.

The thing is, Alex is not a student, he's 29 and has a job, he just still has the student mentality and lives like he's still a teenager.

Alex was sat at his desk tapping away into his laptop, I've no idea what he's doing, he just told me he would do some research.

"Anything?" I asked sipping my tea; it was disgusting so I put the cup down among the many other discarded teas and coffees, all the cups on the floor seemed to be half full, or half empty depending on your point of view.

"Shh, I'm looking". He replied without turning around.

I sighed and looked around the room for something to distract me, I settled on a torn magazine with an article on paranormal investigations.

Reading the article it detailed a group who had all disappeared whilst investigating a supposed haunted house in America. The team had gone in all fired up with cameras filming everything they did but they were never seen again and all the footage came out as just static.

The article teased that it knew what had happened and turn to page 12 to find out the truth, I did so, only to find page 12 had been torn out to make filters for joints.

I threw the magazine on the floor and sighed again.

Alex spun around in his chair and said "Okay, I think I have someone who can help!"

"Really? How?" I asked suspiciously.

"Well, I couldn't find any reference specifically to six legged talking cats that hide in secret tunnels inside sheds, but I did find a guy who specializes in the weird and unusual, and he lives about an hour's drive from here."

"Did you just Google *six legged talking cats that hide in secret tunnels*?" I asked

"Of course, what did you think I was doing?" He looked puzzled.

"Never mind, so how do you think this guy can help?"

"He's got all sorts of equipment for investigating the supernatural, I've chatted with him a few times on the paranormal forum and he seems to know what he's doing".

"I don't think this is a ghost thing."

"It's not just ghosts dude, he investigates werewolves, vampires even looked into a leprechaun living under London Bridge."

"Sounds like a nutjob". I rolled my eyes.

"A nutjob is exactly what we need right now!" Alex leapt up and grabbed his jacket.

"Come on, he's replied to my message and says we can come talk with him."

"Ah, fine, whatever. I guess I'll try anything at this stage." I stood up and followed Alex outside.

We climbed into Alex's battered old Jeep he shoved a cassette into the deck by some band I had never heard of and set off.

"We need petrol first, um, you okay paying?" Alex looked at me sheepishly

"I suppose, just petrol though, we don't need anything else!"

Alex smiled, twenty minutes later we were drinking slushies' and munching on petrol station snacks. I'm too weak willed when it comes to impulse buys.

I settled back in my seat chucking the empty M & M's bag into the back seat where it joined a thousand other junk food wrappers. I closed my eyes and thought about everything that had happened.

8

"Jack....Jack...wake up. We've arrived at Disneyland!" Alex was rudely jabbing me awake with his car keys.

"OK, OK, I'm awake, where's Dumbo?" I went to rub my eyes and poked myself in my left eye with my stub.

"Ow, dammit"

"Idiot" Laughed Alex "Anyway we're at Kevin's place".

"You *sure* his name is Kevin?" I looked at him, one eyebrow raised.

"Of course! Come on lets go inside".

We exited the car and I found we were stood in front of what I could only describe as a 'weirdy beardy' store. If you are unfamiliar with the term it's a shop that sells things like incense burners, skull themed decorations, tarot cards, books on witchcraft...you get the idea. There's one in every town, usually hidden away from the main street shops.

"Well this is definitely the place" I said as we pushed the door open setting off a ring from a little bell.

Inside was as I expected, dark and cramp, shelves bursting with oddities and the inevitable reek of incense that would surely live on long after the store had been bought out and turned into a mini Tesco.

To my surprise instead of the usual sound of wind chimes and sea sounds some rather tasteful classical music was playing over the shops speaker system.

We wove our way through the shop to the counter just as the largest man I had ever seen stepped through a beaded curtain.

"Ah greetings my young fellows! How can I help?" Kevin had a posh accent with just a hint of South African to it; he was as bald and black as an eight ball and must have been at least six foot six and built like an American wrestler, I thought Alex was tall but this man towered over him.

"Hey, it's me, sexbombchocolate83, Alex" Alex said extending his hand.

I knew Alex well enough to know that was his online username.

"Ah my friend! It's good to finally meet you!" Kevin shook Alex's hand heartily. "And you my friend?" He turned to me and reached out his hand again.

"Hi, I'm Jack" I went to shake his hand with my remaining one.

"Nice to meet you Jack, my name is Calvin" Calvin said gripping my hand tight, I glared at Alex who just shrugged.

Calvin's grip was so tight I couldn't resist and as he shook my hand I let it release leaving this giant of a man stood holding a severed hand.

The look on his face was a priceless mix of surprise and abject fear. Alex and I knew this routine and were both smirking. Then Calvin suddenly burst into booming laughter, tears flowing down his cheeks.

"Oh my friend! Alex told me about your.....condition? But to see it for myself is something else!"

"Sorry if I freaked you out, I just couldn't help myself. Would you mind giving me my hand back now though, feel kind of naked with no hands." I said

"Of course dear chap, here show me how it works." He tried to pass my hand back to me but I had nothing to grab it with.

"If you hold it by the finger and line the wrist up with my stump I'll show you"

He did as instructed and as the hand came into contact with my stump the two of them fused together with ease, he let go amazed and I wiggled my fingers.

"See, easy" I said, glad to have a hand back.

"Amazing, simply amazing!" Calvin was examining my hand and wrist "You can't even see a join, it must be so useful!"

"Not really, apart from the handshake gag I've yet to really find a use for it." I shrugged.

"Hmm, I suppose not. Still amazing all the same. Come join me in the parlour and we can discuss your predicament" Calvin motioned for us to follow him through the beaded curtain.

He led us into the back room of the shop were a small kitchenette stood; there was a small table with seating for two in the middle of the room. Seated at one side of the table was a woman immersed in a crossword, in contrast to Calvin's black as night skin she was so pale she was almost ashen. As we entered she looked up to see us.

"Oh these must be the guys you were telling my about" she stood up and eyed us both, she smiled but there was a sadness in her eyes and it looked like she had been recently crying. "Hi, I'm Isabella, Calvin's wife", she was much shorter than Calvin (then again most people would be).

"More than my wife, Izzy is also my assistant in all things supernatural". Calvin said proudly hugging his wife who looked like she would be engulfed in his mass.

"Nice to meet you" Alex and I both said in unison, and for some reason Alex bowed. Confused Isabella nodded and sat back down.

Calvin motioned for me to take the other seat and he and Alex leant against the kitchen counter.

"Now please explain fully what has happened thus far while I prepare us some tea" Calvin said and proceeded to get four cups from a small cupboard above the sink. "Do not leave any details out; I must know the whole story."

I started at the beginning, from waking up with a missing hand and went into full detail about the shed, the cat, the tunnel and the time jump. During which Calvin served us chai tea with some hob nob biscuits.

When I had finished I sat back in my chair and stuck a hob nob into my mouth, Alex was busy dunking his into his tea, he pulled out his phone and showed Calvin and Isabella the video he had taken in the tunnel.

Calvin contemplated for a while and then said "A six legged talking cat is certainly outside the scope of my usual expertise but I may know something of this metal tunnel you have encountered."

"Really?" I asked, leaning forward.

"Indeed, it's not something I have much experience with but I have come across such a tunnel during my investigations when I was travelling in Asia." Calvin rubbed his considerable chin.

"I remember that too" Said Isabella "Bangkok wasn't it?"

"That's correct my dear. We were investigating rumours of people disappearing and our search led us to an alley behind a run-down hotel. There we found a small room with just such a tunnel in it." Calvin continued.

"Did you go in? What did you find?" I asked, excited that this was not an isolated incident.

"Hmm" Calvin was deep in thought "I can't seem to remember, Izzy do you recall what happened after we found the tunnel?"

"Now that you mention it, no, my memory is a blank from the moment we entered the tunnel until we were leaving our hotel to fly back home. How weird" Isabella was visibly confused.

"That definitely sounds like the same sort of tunnel we encountered, it seems everyone's memory is affected differently by the experience" I said.

"Well we have a shared experience now, as a team we will crack this case and return your missing appendage to you!" Calvin was excited.

"What I propose" he continued "Is you allow me a day to do some research and prepare, then we shall meet at this public house you mention to further discuss our plans, does this sound amenable to you chaps?"

"Yeah I can work with that, Jack?" Alex looked at me.

"I guess so, I don't really want to put anyone out just for my hand" I said.

"Nonsense! This is what we do, my curiosity is most piqued by this phenomenon and I must know more!" Calvin boomed.

"I must admit I am curious too, especially since remembering that tunnel in Thailand which we never got to the bottom of." Isabella said.

"Then it's decided, shall we say 7pm at the Duck and Goose tomorrow night?" Alex was excited at the prospect of an adventure, and also he liked going to the pub.

"Indeed, I shall begin my research immediately and tomorrow we shall formulate a plan, message me the address later." Calvin raised his tea cup towards us all; Alex and Isabella chinked their cups with his and I half-heartedly joined in, an uneasy feeling that this was not going to end well.

We all left the kitchen area together and went back into the shop; Alex was looking over the array of items on sale, he picked up a small mangy looking doll and examined it.

"How much for this?" He asked Calvin.

"Oh that is an ancient Mayan doll, very rare my friend, £12.99 to you" Calvin laughed.

"I'll take it! Um...Jack?" He looked at me trying to adopt puppy dog eyes.

"Ugh, fine I'll pay for it." I took out my wallet and handed Calvin my card.

"A pleasure doing business with you my good chap" He said as he handed me the card back, he put the doll into a paper bag and handed it to me, I handled it like you would a dog poop bag and gave it straight to an excited Alex.

"Thanks Jack!" He beamed and hugged the bag to his chest like a child who has just been given a new action figure.

"Well, thanks for everything Calvin, I look forward to seeing you tomorrow night" I said and lifted my hand so shake his.

Calvin roared with laughter again "Ah ha not this time my friend! Fool me once and all that".

I laughed back "Fair enough! Goodbye for now Calvin."

We all said out farewells and Alex and I got back in the car and he set the sat-nav for home.

9

I never really learned exactly what the facility I was examined in was called or what it was even there for so I will simply refer to it as "The Facility", I assumed it was to study people with abilities like me but in all the years I spent there I never saw anyone outside of the staff and I never heard talk of any person being able to do what I could do or similar.

I was given my own room and could have anything I wanted, games consoles, a massive TV, stereo system, mini fridge stocked with Coca-Cola and root beer (one of the staff was American and he got me hooked onto to it.). Anything I could think of they would provide, as long as my parents agreed and that I continued to allow them to study me.

A personal tutor was provided so I wasn't missing out on important school years, I liked Miss Barden and although the lessons were not of great interest to me they provided a break from the boredom of sitting still while tests were carried out. My arms looked like a junkies with all the needle marks from the multiple times my blood was taken.

My parents would visit several times a week and I was allowed out at weekends for day trips on the agreement that we would return and not mention anything about the facility to anyone outside of it. A bodyguard/spy was always a few steps behind us wherever we went. His name was Steve and we became friends of a sort, as close to friends as a fully grown man and a twelve year old could be anyway. I relished our days out when I could spend time with both my parents and Steve, who would be the one to bring me back to my room and often stay to play the latest Call Of Duty game with me.

As time went on the tests became less and less and days could go by without any of the doctors seeing me, I spent my time studying with my tutor and playing video games with Steve who had at this point been appointed my official guardian. It seemed like the scientists and military men who roamed the halls of the facility had given up on me.

Much as I enjoyed playing video games and watching movies my favourite activity during my time at the facility was exploring the small woods that surrounded the building. The whole area was fenced off and guarded so no one could get in or out, this meant I was allowed free roam of the woods, as long as I returned for my scheduled appointments with my tutor or one of the doctors which were getting less and less. I spent much of my free time in those woods, doing nothing more than watching nature unfold, squirrels and birds fascinated me and I could sit and watch them go about their business for hours, remaining totally still so as not to alert them to my presence. I would watch the changing of the seasons, the leaves turning brown and then dropping off, winter bringing frost and sometimes snow and spring starting the whole process off again. I can honestly say my time alone in those woods was when my state of mind was at its most calm, all my anxieties seem to fade away and I found peace. It wasn't just a collection of trees and fauna, to me it was the only place I felt at home.

After having lived in that place for nearly five years I was told I was going to be able to go home, evidently the staff at the facility had come to the conclusion my ability did not hold the secrets to regrowing limbs or whatever it was they were looking for. My parents and I had to sign a disclaimer stating we would not mention anything about the facility and what had occurred there and as long as I was willing to come back in should they ever call I was allowed to go back to live with my parents. We all agreed to the deal and I said goodbye to the facility and more importantly to the woods surrounding it, vowing I would return to them some day.

10

Driving back from Calvin's', Alex asked me about the shop.

"Pretty cool right?" He said grinning.

"Yeah, Calvin seems cool and I like his shop, lots of weird stuff" I replied.

"I know right, skulls and shit...oh dude did you see that giant Dracula statue?"

"Yeah, but vampires don't really do it for me" I shrugged

"How come? I think vampires are cool!"

"Well I think it's down to the movies and the way they can be dealt with"

"Go on" Alex prompted.

"OK, so you know they can be killed by decapitation or a stake to the heart right?"

"Of course"

"Right, but that would also kill anybody, but with vampires you've then got daylight which will kill them, plus their aversion to garlic, running water and crucifixes. I mean if all that's true they are pretty easy to avoid" I continued.

"Well when you put it like that" Alex laughed.

"Garlic! It's a bloody vegetable! Imagine warding off a werewolf with a turnip!

"I'll have to ask Calvin if any of it is true".

"I don't think vampires actually exist mate" I said

"We'll see! We'll see!" Alex grinned back at me "Ooh I nearly forgot!"

Alex reached behind him and pulled out the hideous doll he had got me to buy for him, he sat it on the dash board, it stared at us with dead beaded eyes. It was about three inches tall and looked like it was carved from wood and limbs made from various bones sewed onto it, I hoped they were animal bones.

"Why on earth did you want that?" I asked, pointing at the doll.

"I think it's cool! Don't you think it's cool?" He replied.

"I think it's creepy. It's eerily familiar somehow and I think it's watching me." I shivered

"It wants to eat your soul! Bwa ha ha!" Alex evil laughed and patted the doll on its head "Who knows, maybe it will bring us good luck?"

"Maybe. Or maybe it's just a nasty looking doll, is that real human hair it's got?"

"I dunno, probably" Alex shrugged "Mayans were no doubt into all sorts of weird things."

"I doubt it's actually an ancient Mayan doll, probably some tourist souvenir Calvin picked up on his travels."

"No way mate! This here is your genuine voodoo doll, probably thousands of years old"

"Of course it is" I sighed "Still think it's creepy whatever it is."

"You'll get used to it....I need to pee, I'm going to pull over at this petrol station" Alex flicked the indicator and pulled into the forecourt.

"Get snacks!" I yelled as he was getting out of the car, he waved at me to acknowledge my request.

I flicked through the apps on my phone and settled on a mundane game of solitaire, being an easy game to play one handed, as I was playing from the corner of my eye I noticed the Mayan doll's head turn ever so slightly towards me.

I dropped the phone and stared at the doll, had it moved? Maybe just fell slightly giving the illusion of movement? Just as I had resigned myself to the fact I was imagining things, the doll winked at me.

11

Alex invited me in when we got back but I said I was knackered and would just drive my car home.

I hadn't mentioned the doll to Alex, I was freaked out but wasn't convinced I hadn't just imagined the whole thing; the doll certainly hadn't done anything else the whole trip home. I should know, I stared at that thing till my eyes dried out!

Before going upstairs I popped into the Asian supermarket that currently took up the retail space below my flat.

The shopkeeper was using his best Chinese accent whilst chatting to a customer, I knew it was put on because I'd become quite friendly with him ever since he took over the shop. His name was Martin and he came from Winchester, his great, great, great grandparents may have come over from China but that was as close to Asian as he got. Martin apparently lived in the flat opposite mine above the shop but I had never seen anyone go in or out of that door, he always seemed to be working.

I went over to the fridge which displayed an abundance of weird and colourful cans of fizzy pop; I long ago discovered that if you want proper American root beer the best place to get it is an Asian supermarket. I don't know why they stock a most decidedly non-Asian drink but they all seem to sell it. I grabbed a can of A&W and walked over to the counter, the previous customer was just leaving the store.

"Morning Martin" I said, putting the can on the counter.

"Morning Jack, how's things, whoa what happened to your hand?" Martin asked, dropping the accent and slipping back into his south England tongue.

"That's a long story, I don't think you'd believe me even if I told you" I said sighing.

"Fair enough! Just the root beer today?" He scanned the can through his till.

"Yes thanks, just that today" I handed him a couple of pound coins.

"You should really try some of the other drinks we have; some of them are pretty good you know." Martin handed me my change.

"Better then root beer?" I smiled

"Well, not to someone who loves root beer like you do!" He laughed "Hey I've got something else for you" Martin handed me a bunch of small packets with Japanese writing all over them.

"What are these?" I asked looking at the packets.

"Some kind of Japanese snack, not really sure what, my Japanese is about as good as my Chinese" He gave me a knowing wink "I never sell any so figured you may as well have them, I know your friend likes weird stuff".

"Well thanks...I guess" I shoved the packets into my pocket, just then a customer came in and he slipped seamlessly into his Asian persona to greet them, he winked at me again and I nodded goodbye and left the shop.

Back in my flat I stuck the TV on and sat on the bed drinking my root beer. I got a packet of the weird looking snacks out of my pocket and opened them up, not easy with one hand by the way. Immediately I was hit with a rancid fish smell, inside was what looked like crisps, I figured maybe it was some kind of Japanese take on fish and chips.

I stuck one in my mouth and bit down, then instantly spat it out into my hand, it tasted like dried fish. Not a nice tasting fish either, like somebody got some dead rotting fish and freeze dried them. I threw the rest of the pack in the bin and took a large swig of my root beer to try to get rid of the taste.

On the TV couples were competing for who could make the most profit selling antiques they found at car boot sales. I muted the TV and played some music on my phone, I lay back on the bed, slowly I fell asleep and dreamt of six legged cats and evil looking dolls.

12

I spent most of Sunday doing bugger all, watched a movie, tried to play some video games but quickly realized controllers are not designed for the single handed, generally I just dossed around until evening rolled around, I threw a coat on and walked to the Duck and Goose to meet up with the others.

Walking in to the pub I looked around and saw Calvin and Isabella sat at a booth, Calvin's huge frame taking up almost half a booth to himself, he saw me, stood up and called over to me.

"Jack! My friend, come join us!" He waved me over, the whole pub turned to look at the giant black man shouting, I say the whole pub, there was only a scattering of customers along with the landlord and the barmaid. It was a nice pub but it had seen better days, Alex and I liked it because it was rarely busy so you could always get a good seat and no queues at the bar.

I went over to the booth "Can I get anyone a drink before I sit down?" I asked.

"We have our beverages but please go get yourself whatever your chosen tipple is, I have opened a tab at the bar for us all" Calvin replied.

"Are you sure?" I asked

"Of course, of course! Go, indulge yourself" Calvin waved me away so I went to the bar and ordered a pint of bitter.

I sat down in the booth opposite Calvin and Isabella.

"Thanks for this" I said raising my glass.

"The pleasure is mine" Calvin replied.

"Hi Jack, where is your friend Alex?" Isabella asked.

"Hi Isabella, Alex is running late, as usual. Actually I'm glad to have a moment alone with you two, there's something I wanted to ask you."

"Please, go ahead, ask us anything" Calvin leaned forward curious.

"Well it's about that doll Alex bought, well I bought technically" Calvin laughed as I continued "Where did you get it? Is it really Mayan?"

Calvin laughed even harder "Oh my friend, do you really think an ancient Mayan artefact would sell for £13? No no, I don't even think Mayan's used voodoo dolls, although they did carve effigies to their gods; it's just a novelty souvenir, one of a thousand. I picked it up Greece on holiday, thought it might sell well in the shop but it's been sat on the shelf for years with no takers, until your colleague took a shine to it."

"I see, so it's not got any um…spiritual meaning or anything?" I asked sheepishly

"Not that I am aware, why did something happen with the doll?" Calvin asked.

I was considering how to answer that when Alex came in through the main door and shouted over to us "Drinks lady and gents?"

"I'll tell you later" I said, not really sure that I would.

We all had our drinks and made idle chatter for a few minutes before the topic at hand came up, Calvin's face went from jovial to serious as he leant in to tell us what he had learnt.

"As far as I can ascertain tunnels like this have appeared all over the world, but anyone who has had experience with them has a very hazy memory regarding the whole affair. There are various reports of people finding the tunnels but never any follow up. It seems, Jack my friend, you are the first person to have entered one of these tunnels and not totally lost your memory."

"So we have no idea what the tunnels are and where they go?" I asked.

"Not exactly, no." Calvin said "But from my research and due to the nature of these tunnels we can assume they act as some kind of portal"

"A portal?" Alex asked "To where?"

"That my friend is the mystery!" Calvin replied and sat back.

"No offence Calvin but this sounds a little far-fetched to me; I mean magical portals that go who knows where?" I said.

12

"It may seem unreal but compared to the many supernatural events we have experienced a portal is not that odd" Isabella said.

Calvin nodded "indeed, indeed. After all you yourself have witnessed a six legged talking cat and experienced the effects the portal has on humans, surely your mind has been opened to a wider world then the one we all experience?"

I thought for a while, I had seen things this weekend that couldn't possibly be explained rationally.

"OK, so let's say it is a portal" I said after a moment "How do we go about getting my hand back?"

"We could blow it up!" Alex suggested

"I don't think that would achieve anything, in fact that might cause a catastrophic disaster, no no, we need a much subtler approach" Calvin replied, rubbing his chin.

"We have a plan, well the beginnings of a plan" Isabella said "First I think we should all go and see this shed where the tunnel is located."

We took our drinks and headed outside to the patio area of the pub, it was currently empty of customers, not many smokers left and too cold to be sat outside.

Alex immediately started vaping, this time the smell of aniseed and strawberries, one of his slightly more pleasant concoctions. "This is the shed of doom" Alex said knocking on the shed door.

"I see" Calvin said walking around the shed examining it thoroughly "Nothing out of the ordinary from the outside, a perfectly normal looking storage facility, shall we open it?"

"I guess we have to" I said and looked at the latch on the door; the padlock was still in the wrong place and thus was totally useless in doing its one job. Tentatively I opened the door, half expecting to reveal some parasols and perhaps a spade or garden tools, but no, the metal tunnel was there in all its shiny glory,

"Well, well, well" Said Calvin "It's as I suspected but is still fascinating to see it for myself".

"It's bringing back memories from that time in Bangkok, it's still fuzzy in my mind but this certainly looks like what I can remember."

Calvin nodded, then slowly shut the door and put the latch back on.

"So what now?" Alex asked.

"Now" Calvin started "Jack and I need to go in".

I gasped "What? We know what happens when we go in, time resets and everyone but me forgets, we'll be back at stage one before we even met."

"Ah that is where my research comes into play; see I have concocted a talisman of sorts, one that should negate the effects of the tunnel". Calvin pulled out a large locket on a chain from within his briefcase.

"Whoa, that's awesome!" Said Alex, exhaling his vapour.

"Will it work?" I asked "Will we be able to get through the tunnel?"

"Sadly this is not an exact science my friend, I cannot attest to the efficiency of the talisman, only that my research indicates it can provide resistance to the supernatural."

"There's no guarantee it will work as we expect but it's all we have" Isabella said.

"Good enough for me!" Said Alex

"You go in then!" I replied.

"No, I'm afraid it must be you who goes with me Jack" Calvin said.

"How come?" I asked

"Because if the talisman fails we need your ability to remember so we can start again, it will be a pain getting us all back together but it's better than starting completely from scratch as when you awoke to find you were missing an appendage" Calvin explained.

I contemplated for a moment "I guess we have to try, I just don't fancy doing all this again!" I sighed "So when do we go?"

"No time like the present!" Alex said, I glared at him.

"Our friend is correct, we may as well try it now, this time we will have Alex and Izzy on the outside keeping watch." Calvin said, Isabella nodded.

"Okay, I suppose we may as well get it over with" I steeled myself for what was to come.

"Very well, here you take this amulet" Calvin handed me the talisman and proceeded to take a second one from his case which he put around his neck.

I put the chain around my neck and examined the locket, it stank.

"Jeez what is that smell?"

Isabella laughed "It's a special mixture of various sources; you don't really want to know"

"Fair enough" I lowered the locket, Calvin pulled out an industrial sized torch which he handed to me and another for himself.

"I think we are as prepared as we can be" He said "Are you ready my friend?"

"I guess so, let's get it over with" I replied, hoping the talismans would work but still not convinced of their power. Still, stranger things had happened in the past 24 hours so who was I to doubt the existence of magic.

Calvin stood in front of the shed, I got behind him, torch clasped in my remaining hand.

"You both ready?" Isabella asked her hand on the door latch.

"Let's do this!" I said with more enthusiasm then I actually felt, Calvin simply nodded.

"Good luck guys!" Alex spoke in a cloud of vapour.

Isabella eased the door open and Calvin began to walk into the tunnel with me creeping behind his giant form.

13

When I moved back in with my parents that cold November after leaving the facility they had already decorated the house for Christmas, tinsel was everywhere and a huge tree took up most of the living room. The house had changed somewhat, newly decorated, new furniture and a new modern kitchen. It turns out the government had been sending my parents monthly cheques whilst I was in the facility, these cheques would continue as long as we kept our mouths shut.

Only my room was unchanged since I left, I was an only child so had no siblings to claim my space. Snoopy curtains hung in the windows, space themed wallpaper lined the walls, it all seemed so childish to me at the tender age of 15, mum and dad agreed I could get all new stuff to make it more 'me', they could afford it all now with the government money coming in.

It was too far into the school year for me to go back into the system so the personal tuition with Miss Barden continued, besides I was at a level far beyond other kids my age, having had one-on-one lessons and nothing much else to do but study for the past few years.

I took my exams in January at a private facility and did pretty well, I wasn't a genius or anything but I was smart and advanced for my age. Due to my good results it was agreed I could start college and be back in with other students in September when the new term started.

That first year out of the facility was spent mainly alone in my room, all my friends had grown up without me and moved on with their lives and my social skills were severely hampered by not having interacted with anyone my own age for years. I missed visiting the woods and although I tried to recreate the experience by visiting local forests, it was never the same, there was always people walking their dogs or just going for a stroll and I could never find the peace I had found in those woods outside the facility.

Steve, the bodyguard from the facility, would come and visit on occasion and we would hang out but his visits became less and less frequent as the year went on and eventually he stopped coming altogether.

The internet became my lifeline, it allowed me to interact with strangers without having to leave the house, I became pretty reclusive and my parents started to worry about me. I assured them I was fine but I was slowly slipping into a depressive state.

Eventually I was taken to a regular doctor, of course we couldn't explain what had happened to me in my young life so my parents made up some story about how I found it hard to make friends and be sociable. The doctor dutifully supplied me with anti-depressants; I rejected the offer of counselling as I had spent enough time with psychiatrists to last a life time.

If you've never had full blown depression (I mean more than just feeling sad) it's hard to explain how crippling it is. Everything seems like an effort, you want to be alone all the time but then your own thoughts can work against you, I was going through the motions of being a normal teenager but inside I was messed up. Which in hindsight *is* kind of like a normal teenager, sadly my angst would go on for many years.

After a few weeks on the meds I began to improve my mental health somewhat, I wasn't exactly a social butterfly but I was able to visit café's and go shopping alone without experiencing a panic attack sometimes, however I would often chicken out at the last minute or make some excuse to myself that I required me to leave.

My anxiety grew worse as the start date of college neared but I was determined to go and get out of the funk I had settled into. That September I turned up to college half expecting to collapse in a heap and never go back.

14

The next thing I knew after entering the portal with Calvin was waking up in my bed, cursing; I looked at my phone, it was 6pm Sunday night, I had gone back in time only a couple of hours this time. As I went to put my phone down it buzzed with a text message from Calvin, it just said two words

I remember

Relief washed over me, I was no longer alone in this, I text back to say I too remembered and would meet him at the pub as before, jumped in the shower and walked briskly to the pub.

Inside I was greeted once again by Calvin and Isabella; Calvin smiled and bid me to sit down.

"I have explained the situation to Izzy" He started "Luckily she is understanding of such experiences and did not doubt me for a moment".

"That's good" I said "And I am so pleased to have someone else remember this, I guess the talismans worked?"

"To a certain extent, it allowed me to retain my memory of the whole affair but did not allow us further entry into the tunnel." Calvin replied.

"We suspect we are going to need stronger protection to navigate the portal" Isabella said, as she spoke Alex arrived through the doors of the pub, oblivious to the fact we had all done this before.

He sat with us and between the three of us we explained in detail what had happened early in the day, or later, depending on your point of view! He sat back for a moment.

"I'm going to need a bigger drink, anyone else?" He said standing, we all nodded and Alex went to the bar to get a round in, putting it on Calvin's tab of course.

After getting our drinks and all having a hearty sip of them, Alex almost finishing half his pint in one gulp he spoke up.

"So what can we do to get through the portal?"

"Calvin has a plan, but it's not going to be easy" Isabella said "and there is no guarantee it will work any better, but it's all we currently have to try"

"OK, let's hear this plan then" I said

Calvin took another deep sip of his brandy and looked at Alex and I intently,

"We are going to need the cat" he said, solemnly

"Excuse me?" Said Alex

"The six legged talking cat?" I asked

Calvin nodded, "Indeed, it is my belief that this cat must possess something that allows it to traverse the portal without time resetting on it, also I don't think it's actually a cat"

"Well it certainly looked like a cat" I said "Apart from the extra legs, oh and the fact it spoke"

"Exactly, cats, as we are all aware, do not generally speak, at least not in a language we can understand. There are various studies suggesting they communicate with other felines but that is an entirely different matter." Calvin shook his head.

"OK, so if it's not a cat, what is it?" I asked

"That is currently a mystery, I have my suspicions but until these are confirmed I don't care to speculate. Suffice to say, whatever it is, we need it. It is the key to the portal, so to speak" Calvin sat back and sipped from his brandy once more.

I had no reason to doubt Calvin's theory; the man knew far more than me regarding these matters after all, we all remained silent for a few moments, the only sounds being the slurping of drinks and the mumbled chatter from the few other customers at the pub. Eventually Isabella spoke

"We are going to have to try and capture this 'cat' somehow, to do that we need to lay a trap".

"How do we know the cat will even come back?" Alex asked.

"Ah that is where technology comes into play, see earlier today, Isabella and I visited this pub and setup a small camera out the back facing the shed". Calvin pulled his phone out and pulled up some videos. "We set the camera to record on the sensing of motion, as you can see here is the landlord of the pub emptying the ash trays" He held out the phone so we could see the video, it wasn't the best quality but it was clear enough to see man's arms just in shot as he took the full ashtrays and replaced them with clean ones.

"And now this" Calvin swiped to another video, at first we couldn't see anything but then a blur shot across the screen".

"That could be anything" I said "Can you slow it down?"

"Better than that my friend, I have managed to pause the video, zoom in and, somewhat sharpen the image" he took the phone back and switched to photos then turned it back to us. There right in the centre of frame was a blob of ginger fur, it was fuzzy and hard to make out but it was clearly the shape of a cat.

I sat back. "Wow, so it does exist"

"Of course, did you doubt your own eyes young Jack?" Calvin asked.

"I was beginning to" I said "So we know the cat is still out there, how do we know when it comes and goes?"

"Yeah what if it only comes out on odd occasions?" Alex asked.

"Ah but you see there is more than one video, in fact we managed to capture an image of the cat another two times in the space of the three hours the camera was installed." Calvin smiled.

"I see, well that is interesting, clearly this cat is up to something" I said.

"Indeed, and this presents us with an opportunity to ensnare the feline and use it for our purposes" Calvin put his phone away.

"So how do we do that?" Alex asked, excited at the prospect of an adventure.

"We have a plan for that as well, although you might not like it" Isabella said. She continued explaining the plan to us, when she was finished I slumped in my seat.

"Ugh, alright, I'll do it" I said.

15

Inside the wheelie bin was dark. Dark and smelly. We had managed to find an empty one but it still retained the smell of various rubbish. I crouched inside trying to keep as silent as possible to remain undetected. The plan we had now put in motion involved me being in here so I could be near the action without the cat being aware of anything amiss. I had my phone in my one hand, switched to silent mode, ready to receive a message that the plan was a go. I felt ridiculous huddled up in a rubbish bin but I understood I was the only one who would fit, and even then, only after I detached my entire left arm at the shoulder. It afforded me the extra space I needed; we discussed removing a leg as well but realized it may be necessary for me to leap out quickly which would be severely hampered with two missing limbs.

I went over the plan in my mind.

"We'll need some kind of bait". Isabella had said, we all thought for a moment and then it hit me. The stinky fish snacks I had got from Martin were still in my jacket pocket; I pulled them out and offered them around. All agreed they stunk strong enough that any cat would be interested, we just had to hope this particular creature was cat-like enough to find them appealing.

The snacks were spread out over the patio of the pub garden, leaving a trail from the shed to the wheelie bin I now sat in. The idea was once the cat had become distracted with the revolting fish bits I was to leap out and throw a sack over it. The sack was resting on my shoulder for quick access. Meanwhile Alex would lie in wait just inside the pub door, his role was to rush to block the cat from getting back under the shed door should I not be quick enough. He too was armed with a sack, the thinking being that between the two of us we would be able to trap the cat one way or another.

I was beginning to feel foolish sat in here, what if the cat didn't show up? Just how long could we wait before giving up? It feels like I have been in here for hours but it's only been 20 minutes. Calvin had remained inside the pub acting as a bouncer to stop anyone trying to get outside, the landlord had been easily persuaded to accommodate them with a crisp twenty in his hand. Calvin had also promised a second twenty pounds if the landlord agreed not to interfere or ask any questions.

Another ten minutes passed and I was starting to cramp up, I shuffled my legs as much as I could trying to keep silent, just then my phone lit up.

Cat is sniffing bait

I steeled myself, ready to pounce as soon as I received the signal, a minute passed and I though the cat must have not taken an interest in the snacks, then.

GO!

I leapt up, throwing the bin lid open and grasping the sack in my one hand, the cat stopped eating and stared up me, I attempted to exit the bin in a swift jumping movement but it fell over and I ungraciously tumbled out. The cat turned and was about to head to refuge under the shed door but Alex was too quick for him and he was waiting, his own sack in hand. The cat skidded to a halt and looked around for an escape giving me the precious moment I needed to stand up and ready myself. I pushed the bin aside blocking the only exit left.

"Now Alex! Grab it" I yelled.

Alex leapt forward with his sack grasped between both hands but the cat was too fast for him and it easily dodged him and ran towards me, I swung at the cat with my sack, not so easy with one hand (we really should have thought this through), I managed to whack the cat with the sack knocking him over but not enough to stop him, the motion caused him to roll to one side but he was soon up on his feet and running back in Alex's direction. The cat, realizing his way to the shed was blocked by Alex, veered to the left and headed for the wall. We hadn't thought about the cat scaling a seven foot wall to make his escape but that's exactly what he was about to do, without thinking I kicked out as hard as I could letting my foot fly off my body and hurtle towards the cat.

Luck was on our side as my foot, complete with my shoe attached struck the cat halfway up the wall, dazed it fell to the ground, giving Alex the brief moment he needed to throw the sack over the cat and close the opening tight.

The cat struggled against the sack and it seemed he would be free in no time if we didn't hurry.

"Calvin! A little help!" Alex called prompting Calvin to burst through the pub doors armed with a metal cage he had acquired from a local pet shop. It was designed as a training crate for small dogs but met our needs perfectly.

Calvin held open the cage door and Alex stuffed the sacked cat inside, he slammed the door shut and Calvin clipped a padlock in place. The cat was ours.

A car horn honked and we turned to see Isabella pulling up in a large mobile home, she called out the window.

"Quick, get it inside!"

Alex quickly picked up my foot and tossed it to me; I caught it and reattached it to my ankle. Then Alex and I carried the crate between us as Calvin opened the back door to the van to let us in. We took the crate in and set it down in on the floor in-between the two bench seats. I sat down and breathed a sigh of relief, Alex threw a blanket over the cage and did the same.

"One second!" Yelled Calvin as he ran back inside the pub.

"Where's he going?" Alex asked Isabella

"Probably to pay his tab, he likes to settle up his bills straight away" She replied.

"Fair enough" I laughed. I looked around the interior of the mobile home; it was huge inside with ample space for the four of us and provided all the amenities one would need to live by – cooker, microwave, shower, toilet even a decent sized TV mounted in the corner.

Next to Alex lay my left arm, I asked him to pass it to me and reattached it to the shoulder.

Soon Calvin was back with us and he jumped into the passenger seat of the van.

"Let's go my love!" He said and Isabella hit the accelerator and off we went.

"Quick thinking with the foot thing mate." Alex said smiling at me.

"I knew this ability had to be good for something, turns out it's good for knocking down cats" We all laughed together.

"An excellently played operation boys!" Calvin said beaming "Now let's get to a safe space and park up, then we can deal with our feline hostage."

16

My first few weeks at college were, quite frankly, terrifying. I refused to engage with other students and kept myself to myself, only speaking when a tutor asked me a question. I dutifully attended my lessons, having started earlier than most I was the youngest student there and felt more isolated than ever.

One day I was eating my lunch alone as usual on the steps behind the college science buildings where I had discovered almost no one ever came, when I voice interrupted my thoughts.

"Hey Kid!" The voice said; I turned to see a tall lanky student walking over to me; I said nothing but nodded as way of an answer. The man sat down next to me with more confidence than I had ever seen in a teenager.

"Question for you: How do you weigh your own head?" He asked.

"What?" I responded, totally thrown.

"It's something I've been thinking about for a while now, like is there a way you could figure out how much your head weighed on its own, I tried laying on a scale but I'm not convinced that is an accurate reading." He looked at me as if this was a perfectly normal topic of conversation. I paused for a while before speaking up.

"Uh...well...I suppose you could submerge your head in water and measure the amount of water it displaced" I mumbled.

"Interesting. That could work." He said scratching his chin.

"But that would require the head to have the same density of water I suppose which could cause anomalies....why....why do you want to know this?" I asked nervously.

"I dunno, just wondered…I'm Alex by the way" He stuck his hand out and reluctantly I shook it, politeness overtaking anxiety at that moment in time.

"I'm Jack" I said

"Nice to meet you Jack, what you eating?" Alex asked.

"Just a sandwich, cheese and pickle, nothing exciting" I replied lifting up the limp sandwich.

"Boring!" Alex yelled leaping up "Come on, let's go to McDonalds and get a burger" he was walking away before I even had a chance to voice my objections. Then something in me just went 'screw it' and I stood up and followed Alex. It was, as they say, the beginning of a beautiful friendship, also a weird one as it turned out.

17

The camper-van was stopped down an isolated road, pulled over to one side. All the curtains had been drawn and the four of us huddled around the cage, waiting for someone to make a move.

"It's being very quiet" whispered Alex.

"Maybe it's plotting?" said Isabella.

"Maybe it's dead?" I said.

"I'm not dead" came a voice from the cage.

We all looked at each other, Calvin and Alex smiled.

"Shall we?" asked Calvin.

"Let's!" said Alex, Isabella and I merely nodded.

Calvin slowly pulled the blanket from over the cage, the six legged cat was sat upright, having escaped the sack. We all stared, taking in the chance to properly examine the mutated feline in front of us.

"Well?" said the cat "What do you want with me?"

We all knew the cat could talk but it was still a shock to see it right in front of you.

"Greetings, my name is Calvin, we wish to converse with you about my colleagues missing appendage and, perhaps, to learn more about your species. I take it you are not an earthly cat?" Calvin spoke as if chatting with a work colleague rather than some mutant cat.

"Well that's obvious, we are fully aware your earth felines are incapable of speech, despite being smarter than the dominant species of this planet" the cat said.

"He means us right?" said Alex.

"I believe so my friend" Calvin said, to the cat he asked "So you are not of this planet at all?"

"Correct" stated the cat, it began licking it's paws and cleaning itself, it was weird to watch as it used three of its legs at the same time.

"And is this your true form?" Calvin prompted.

"Ha! My true form is incomprehensible to such a stunted race as humanity!" the cat laughed.

"Try us!" Tempted Alex

"Very well" said the cat, it began to change in front of our eyes. No description can do justice to what we saw next, it was impossible to focus on and so overwhelmingly bright it stung my eyes and gave me an instant migraine. In pain I shrieked and closed my eyes tight but the blurry image somehow still managed to penetrate my eye lids. Around me the other three were also screaming in pain. Calvin felt around for the blanket and threw it over the cage.

"Enough!" He yelled. The brightness died down until we were left with spots in our eyes and a throbbing headache.

"I warned you" the cat said from under the blanket "you can uncover me now".

Tentatively Calvin lifted the blanket until he was sure the creature had returned to his cat form, he fully removed the blanket but kept it close to his hand in case it was needed again.

"Well it seems you are certainly not of this earth" Calvin commented "Do you have a name which we can address you by?"

"My real name would split your eardrums and make your brain bleed!" the cat said.

"Try us!" Yelled Alex again.

"Shut up!" Isabella and I shouted at him in unison.

The cat laughed a disturbing sound to say the least "You may call me Tarquin" he said.

Now it was Alex's turn to laugh "Tarquin? Really?" he was covering his mouth.

"It is the name I chose when I arrived on this plane, why does this bring such humour to you?" Tarquin scowled.

"You chose it?" Alex laughed harder.

"Yes, we all choose our names." Tarquin looked like he was sulking.

"Hmm, OK, Tarquin" Alex was trying hard not to laugh. The rest of us were still in too much pain to find it amusing.

"It is a perfectly normal human name, I took it from what you people refer to as television; an antiquated way of receiving entertainment but appears to be the obsession of your race."

Calvin looked at Alex who managed to stop laughing but could not refrain from grinning like an idiot.

"Very well, Tarquin, can you tell us more about your race?" He asked.

Tarquin sighed "I suppose there is little point in refusing, you have seen my true form and somehow some of you appear to be immune to our time wipe device. I will tell you what you want but I have a request first."

"We're not letting you out of that cage." Alex said.

"No I understand that, although I hope when you have heard my story you will be inclined to release me." Tarquin said.

"So what do you want?" I asked.

"Well, do you have any more of those delicious fish based snacks?" Tarquin looked like a kitten begging for food, a mutated six legged kitten but still.

I laughed "Sure I have a couple more bags left!" I rummaged in my pocket and pulled out a bag of the snacks, I went to hand it to Tarquin then stopped. "Um, can you open them? With your paws I mean?" I asked

"I would appreciate if you would open them for me and pass the bag through the bars, please." He pleaded

I saw no reason to deny his request so passed them to Alex who opened a bag up and put it through the cage bars, Tarquin flipped the bag upside down with his mouth, tipping the contents onto the solid floor of the cage, the fish smell hit us instantly and we recoiled in disgust. Tarquin munched away greedily, we could hear him purring as he ate. We waited patiently whilst he finished off every last morsel.

"Delicious" He liked his lips "Thank you, I've no idea why I've been craving fish so much."

Alex and I exchanged glances and mentally agreed not to mention cats and their love of fish. Calvin, who had put a handkerchief to his nose, took it away to test the smell and, deciding it was safe to breathe again, turned to Tarquin.

"So, are you prepared to answer our questions?" He asked

"Of course, what would you like to know?" Tarquin was once again cleaning himself.

"Firstly, where are you from?" Calvin asked.

"Where I come from is complicated. It exists outside of space and time as you understand it. Suffice to say my home dwells outside of the human's concept of the universe."

"So you're an alien?" Alex asked.

"I suppose, but I'm not just from another planet, I am from another plane of existence"

"We'll go with alien" Alex decided.

Calvin was about to ask another question when Alex interrupted him.

"Why do you look like a cat?" He asked

"As I just demonstrated my race cannot be viewed by human eyes without eventually leading to madness and death. As such when we visit another location we adapt to fit the environment." Tarquin explained.

"But why a cat?" Alex asked again.

"A cat was one of the first earthly creature I experienced, we observed that cats were able to come and go wherever they so pleased. Humans appear to be more than willing to accommodate the felines or indeed ignore them when seen on the street."

Alex nodded, seemingly satisfied with the answer, Isabella wanted more information however.

"That makes sense, but why six legs? Did it not occur to you that you would stand out from ordinary cats?" She asked.

"Yes indeed, therein lays the problem we have with your planet. Of all the places we have visited, yours is unique in that we cannot seem to perfect the transformation. We have been working on a serum which will allow us to correctly appear as earth creatures." Tarquin said.

"Is that why you have not chosen the human form?" Calvin asked.

"Exactly" Calvin stated "Whenever we tried to emulate the human form the result was disastrous and we would have immediately been spotted as outsiders."

"Wait" I said "Is that why you took my hand?"

"It is. We discovered you as being unique to your species, at first we suspected you were like us, from another realm, but after studying you it became clear you were merely a human with an unusual ability"

"You've been studying me?" I asked shocked.

"Of course. We have had eyes on you for the past five earth years" Calvin said.

"Five years?!" I gasped

"Yes. Since you moved to your current location we have been observing you and trying to reproduce your ability. When it became clear we would not be able to do that a decision was made to obtain part of you to examine more thoroughly".

I slumped back in my seat. My mind reeling with the new found information that I was the subject of an alien species experiments.

"How exactly did you study young Jack without his knowledge?" Calvin asked.

"We have a spy." Tarquin stated.

"A spy?" Alex chimed in "Is it me? Have I been unknowingly providing you with information on my mate?"

Tarquin laughed. "No, we can't take over a humans mind, our spy resides below his residence."

"Below?" I said "You mean the shop?"

"Indeed. You know him as 'Martin'."

"Martin is an alien?" I shot up in my seat, eyes wide.

"He is one of us yes."

"Wait….he looks normal. I thought you couldn't copy the human form?" I said.

"I said we can't perfect the human form; tell me, have you ever seen Martin come out from behind the counter? Have you ever seen his legs?" Tarquin smirked.

I thought for a moment "well, of course....actually no. He's never been anywhere but behind the counter when I've been in." I was baffled, it's not something you ever think about, seeing someone's lower half or not.

"Exactly, like all of our species when we try to emulate earthly forms, something is incorrect. In my case I have two extra limbs, in Martin's case; he has no human legs, hence why a shopkeeper, behind a counter, was the perfect choice." Tarquin explained.

"So what does he have instead of legs?" Alex asked.

"I believe you would refer to them as tentacles." Tarquin said plainly. As if this was the most normal thing in the world.

"Crazy!" Said Alex

"Perhaps we should move on to the most pertinent question?" Calvin said "Why are you here? On our planet I mean."

"I was wondering when you would get to that" Tarquin smirked.

"Yeah, why invade earth? What did we ever do to you?" Alex said angrily.

"Oh my! Invade you? Is that what you think?" Tarquin was visibly disappointed.

The four of us all exchanged glances before Isabella spoke up.

"Well, yes. Kind of, what else would you be here for?" She said

"I am not here to invade your planet, I am here to save it" Tarquin said.

18

The first time I went to Alex's home I was welcomed with open arms by his parents who seemed almost as eccentric as he did, their house was a shrine to rock and roll, gold records lined the wall and framed signed photos of various rock and roll stars, I had no idea who half of them were but I recognized The Beatles and a few others. Even the furniture looked straight out of the past had a sixties rock and roll vibe, it was very retro and very cool.

Alex was also into rock music but leaned more towards 90's rock, he loved collecting cassette tapes from that era when tapes were at their peak of usage. We would trawl through the charity shops every weekend looking for tapes to add to his collection, often he would bid on eBay auctions and huge boxes of tapes would turn up, he could get them for next to nothing now everyone had moved on to CD's and digital content.

We had great fun going through those boxes and listening to various random tapes on Alex's old fashioned stereo and we discovered many great bands this way that had otherwise disappeared into obscurity, often the tapes would be the type you record over and had no labels indicating what was on them. We liked these the best as you never knew what we were going to hear, usually it was just a copy of an album or a mix tape someone had made but occasionally we would get a tape someone had recorded of themselves.

We would listen to people's home-made attempts at radio shows and plays, comedy sketches and sometimes it sounded like the tape had just been left recording at party, normal conversations coming in as guests must have moved nearer the recorder.

The weirdest one we ever found was a guy's audio diary which started off innocuously enough with his day to day life of restoring a house he had bought but it soon took an eerie turn when he started to document the ghost he thought was haunting the house.

Each entry became more and more creepy as the tape guy described weird noises when no one else was there, appliances turning themselves on and off, sometimes without even being plugged in as well as the smells which he described as "the smell of death".

We listened intently as the hauntings escalated and the guy became deranged on the tape, talking about bleeding walls and visions he had seen, we had no idea how much of it was true but it seemed too real to be made up.

The final entry on the tape was mainly just gibberish followed by some loud bangs and finally a horrifying scream, this was followed by twenty minutes of silence before the tape ran out.

Alex tried to find out who was on the tape by contacting the person he had bought the lot from but they didn't know anything about it, there was no way of finding out whose voice was on the tape or what had happened to him but it started Alex's obsession with the supernatural and he was determined to experience his own haunting.

19

We were driving again, Isabella at the wheel, Calvin in the passenger seat and Alex and I in the back with Tarquin.

The alien cat had explained why his race had come to earth and we were all still in shock. As he told it, his race were not the only dimensional time/space hoppers out there, but they were one of the peaceful advanced races that meant no harm. Others were on such a microscopic level that the human eye would not even be aware if they were here or not, these too meant no harm and were merely explorers.

There was one particular race however who held no such peaceful beliefs; they believed only in chaos and destruction, slashing a wrath of disaster through multiple universes. And apparently, they were headed towards us.

Tarquin went on to explain that, once our universe had become known to those outside of it, this race of beings, which Alex dubbed 'The X-Borgs' when we were unable to even comprehend their true name, had chosen to come here to destroy us. By us, he meant the entire planet Earth. By destroy he meant they would level buildings and either kill or enslave entire species. They had no reason do to this, they didn't need one, it was simply what they did as a species.

Tarquin's species constantly monitored these X-Borgs in an effort to thwart their plans before they could be enacted; he said they had managed to protect multiple planets for the terror of the X-Borgs. When asked if they had ever lost he went very quiet.

"Well, what percentage did you save?" Calvin had asked.

"You must understand it is not an exact figure, merely a speculation on my part" Tarquin had nervously uttered.

"We understand, now please, share with us your speculation." Calvin replied calmly.

"Very well, we have managed to save, approximately, five percent of planets" The cat had stated.

We all say back shocked, Alex was the first to speak.

"Five percent? So you failed ninety five percent of the time??"

"We prefer to dwell on the positives" Tarquin replied, hurt.

"I'd get sacked if I only did five percent of my work!" Alex laughed nervously.

"It's a miracle you haven't been sacked already; I'd say you doing five percent of your work is generous!" I quipped.

Alex laughed harder "That's a fair comment"

We continued to discuss our eminent doom whilst Tarquin tried to allay our fears with his species plans to save us. After some time we were all exhausted from the information we had gathered and all agreed we should take a break. Calvin suggested we drive back to town to gather food and supplies to refuel ourselves before continuing.

We arrived at my flat first and I leapt out whilst the others waited in the van, I was tempted to go into the shop to try and see Martin's tentacle legs but decided I had had enough weirdness for one day. I went upstairs and gathered some clothes and an overnight bag. It had been decided we would all stay in the camper van together, the logic of safety in numbers overriding comfort.

After returning to the van out next stop was a large supermarket, Alex and I agreed to go in and get supplies whilst Calvin and Isabella stayed in the van with Tarquin.

Alex grabbed a trolley and armed with Calvin's credit card we proceeded along the aisles.

"This is fun right?" He said smiling.

"I wouldn't go so far as to call it fun, we might all die!" I replied.

"Well that was always going to happen one day, at least this was we get an adventure out of it. Plus we get a chance to save the world!" Alex was enjoying this far too much but I couldn't help but get caught up in his enthusiasm.

"Does that make us super heroes?" I laughed.

"Sure dude, you can be The Dislocated Man!"

"Yeah, I'm going to say no to that name." I scowled but was grinning really.

"Well we can work on our names; just wish I had a power like you do"

"It's not like it's a great power, we all know how useless it is really" I said

"Ooh look, Reese's!" Alex was easily distracted and the row of orange coloured peanut butter and chocolate treats had caught his eye. He greedily shoved handfuls of the stuff into the trolley.

"I think Calvin meant to get some proper food, not just chocolate" I said.

"This is proper food! It combines sugar, salt, nuts and chocolate...the four food groups" Alex laughed as we carried on through the shop.

We stocked up on cans of pop, bread, milk, eggs, various snacks and a huge jar of instant coffee. I was looking at one of the cans of Coke deep in thought.

"Anything interesting on that can mate?" Alex nudged me out of my trance.

"I was wondering how it was decided that 330 mil was the standard size for a can of pop"

"It is a very specific number isn't it. Maybe it equals a more rounded number in old world measurements?"

"Maybe. Or maybe it's close to a third of a litre?" I contemplated the question for a moment longer "Ah well, I'll Google it later". I put the can in the trolley with the rest of the items.

"I think that'll do." I said, heading for the cashier.

"One more thing, wait here" Alex said and rushed off down the pet aisle.

Back in the van we unloaded the shopping, Calvin showed no interest but Isabella came over to see what we had brought.

"Interesting choices" She said, smiling.

"I knew you'd like them" Alex said, holding out a Reese's bar, Isabella rolled her eyes but took the chocolate anyway and began munching on it.

"Where to now?" She mumbled with her mouth full.

"My place please, need to get my stuff."

Stuff it turns out was a couple of t-shirts and a large bag full of vaping supplies. He also bought the damn doll with him and placed it on the dashboard.

"Ah our good luck charm!" Calvin laughed. I shivered and Tarquin gave me an odd look. I stared back and he nodded as if I should know what he was referring to.

"Well it appears we are all stocked up and ready for adventure, I suggest we park up and rest before Tarquin provides us with more detail." Calvin suggested.

"Would it be possible to be released from the cage? Tarquin politely requested.

"It's hard to know if we can trust you" Isabella said.

Alex chimed in "I have a solution to that!" He delved into the plastic bag from our shopping trip and pulled out a small harness. "It's for walking your cat!" He said triumphantly

"I am a supremely intelligent extra-dimensional being, I don't need a harness!" Tarquin sulkily retorted.

"Yeah, maybe, but I'd feel safer having you on the end of a lead" Alex smiled "Now stay still while I get this on you".

"Aargh, fine! Whatever! Anything to gain your trust so I can get on with my mission!" Tarquin sat back away from the cage door. Calvin assisted Alex in getting the harness on, despite Tarquin surrendering himself to the harness it wasn't easy putting a harness designed for four legged animals onto a six limbed creature, Eventually it was done and Tarquin walked out of the cage.

"Well this is humiliating" He sulked.

"You look great!" Beamed Alex pleased with himself "I also got you some tins of cat food as I wasn't sure what you eat?"

Tarquin's eyes lit up "Oh, um, yes that will suffice, I'll have some now if you don't mind" He tried to hide his enthusiasm but it was clear he had developed a taste fitting with his current form.

20

We were parked up at an almost empty camping ground which allowed us to use the facilities. We all ate well that night and were now sat around feeling stuffed. Calvin was the first to speak.

"Tarquin, would you be able to explain exactly how your race intends to stop these...creatures.."

"X-Borgs!" Alex called.

"Hmm, yes, how will you try to stop these...X-Borgs from carrying out their nefarious plan?" Calvin continued.

"Very well. Of the planets we have managed to save we relied on its dominant species to infiltrate the enemy, this allowed us to sabotage their plans from the inside." Tarquin started.

"How would you infiltrate them?" I asked

"That is why we are trying to perfect human form. On other planets we have had no problem adapting to the local population. This then allows us to infiltrate the areas necessary to obtain what we require." Tarquin explained.

"So you plan to take on human form, how does that allow you access to the X-Borgs? Wouldn't it be easier to turn into one of them?" Alex asked

"Don't be ridiculous, no one can alter their appearance to look like them!" Tarquin said "Once we have adapted to human form we will then allow ourselves to get captured, this will place us in the prime position to stop their plans"

"Oh yeah, sounds much less ridiculous" Alex said rolling his eyes.

"But our plan is being thwarted by something in your human DNA which stops us from successfully assimilating you people." Tarquin continued.

"Yeah I can see how a human turning up with tentacles for legs would cause a few raised eyebrows" I said.

"Exactly. This is why we were so interested in you Jack. A human who could take off and on limbs at will seemed the perfect answer to our issue. If we could replicate your ability we would be able to remove the incorrect appendages and replace them with the correct ones. At least enough to fool the beings until after the mission is complete." Tarquin spoke as if this all made perfect sense. Only Calvin seemed unfazed by it all.

"Yes, I can see how this young man's unique capabilities would be ideal for your situation. Have you had any success examining his hand?" He asked.

"Not as yet. I fear the hand itself does not contain the answers we need" Tarquin lowered his head.

"If not the hand what else do you need?" Isabella asked.

Tarquin looked around then pointed a paw at me "We need him" He said.

21

Later that night Alex, Calvin and Isabella were all asleep, Tarquin curled up next to Alex who had tied the handle of the lead around his wrist. I was unable to sleep, the prospect of being the solution to saving the universe weighing heavy on me. Restless I tossed and turned on my bunk, eventually resigned to lying on my back staring up at the ceiling of the van. Then I heard a noise, a skittering, like a mouse running along the floor of the van, I turned to look but it was dark inside, the only light coming from the moonlight shining in through the wind-shield.

Deciding I was probably imaging things I was about to roll back over when I saw something out the corner of my eye. Suddenly a small figure dashed out from the darkness and I glimpsed it in the moonlight. It was the damn doll. It stood frozen as it realized I could see it. In its hand, looking huge, was a Reese's peanut butter cup. He looked up me and raised a finger to its tiny mouth.

"Shh" it whispered then disappeared back into the darkness. I sat bolt upright and was about to turn on a light and alert the others when I was shushed from another voice, I turned around and could dimly see Tarquin shaking his head at me.

"What the hell is that?" I whispered.

"Keep it down" Tarquin said softly, "take me outside and I will explain, I need to urinate anyway." Reluctantly I undid the lead from Alex's wrist, he stirred but did not wake, I lead Tarquin out the van door and we made our way far enough from the camper to not be heard. Tarquin immediately squatted down to pee.

"Look away please" He said, I looked the other way until he informed me he had finished.

"Now, what is that doll thing?" I asked.

"It's nothing to be afraid of, actually the fact it has revealed itself to you is a good sign. You see that doll is possessed with the soul of another universe hopping creature"

"Oh well that *does* sound like a good thing" I said sarcastically.

"It is, this particular race does no harm, and in fact they are here to help." Tarquin continued

"Help how? By eating our food and scaring the crap out of me?"

"Not at all. It *is* unfortunate it has taken such an unpleasant appearing host but its intentions are purely honourable. It's races purpose is to appear when it senses a major event occurring, they visit planets outside of their own universe and choose one being. They reward that being with a gift."

"A gift? Like a store card or a dead mouse or something?"

"No, no. This gift will imbibe the recipient with a unique special ability. I originally thought you had already been on the receiving end of such a creature but you were born with your ability so it is not the same"

"Wait, so it gives someone superpowers?"

"Exactly" Tarquin stated "They choose one member of the planet's dominant species and reward them with a power."

"What sort of power?" I asked

"Could be one of any number of things, the power of flight, invisibility, anything really."

"So how do they choose the one who gets it?"

"That is not known" Tarquin shook his head.

"Am...am I the chosen one?" I asked

"It would appear so, but you must not reveal your knowledge of this creatures' existence. Doing so could cause it to leave this vessel and look elsewhere for the one."

"So I have to ignore the creepy living doll?"

"Basically, yes. But the doll is not alive as you or I understand it, it is simply a host body for the creature to inhabit until it has served its purpose" said

Tarquin "Now, can we go back to sleep?"

"I guess" I was shaking my head in awe "This has been the weirdest few days of my life"

"You learn to deal with it" Tarquin shrugged his shoulders the best he could for a cat.

"Yeah, not sure I will" I said and walked Tarquin back to the camper, as we entered Alex was awake.

"Where have you guys been?" He asked wearily

"I had to urinate and you appeared to be dead to the world" Tarquin answered, exchanging a quick glance with me.

"Fair enough, could do with a piss myself." Alex stood up and left the van.

"Remember. Say nothing" Tarquin whispered curling up on the bunk. I lay down as well, keeping the lead in my one hand although I felt that Tarquin could escape any time he wanted to. Before I closed my eyes I took a good look around the van, I could just see the doll sat back on the dashboard as if it had never moved. I nodded to it, rolled over and finally sleep hit me.

22

Spending time with Alex that first year of college greatly increased my confidence, his enthusiasm was contagious and I found myself going out more and more. I wouldn't say I made lots of new friends but I wasn't as socially awkward any more and could attend parties and functions without panicking; as long as Alex was with me and as long as I had an exit strategy. Alex was very understanding of my anxiety and would always back me up if I gave him the sign I needed to get out.

We became close friends, he was a couple of years older than me but he was much more immature and his antics made me laugh more than I ever had, he was always getting up to what he called 'adventures' which usually involved breaking into abandoned houses to look for ghosts. We never really found anything but that didn't deter Alex from continuing to try.

He subscribed to multiple online forums where like-minded individuals could share experiences and places worth checking out. It was here he found out about a house in Surrey about 30 miles from where we lived, supposedly many of his online acquaintances had experienced supernatural events at this location.

"Road trip?" He said turning to me explaining what he had read, I was not a believer in ghosts or the supernatural but we always had fun on our days out so I agreed to go.

Alex had recently got his driving license and had managed to get a beat up old Ford escort which he lovingly dubbed The Mystery Machine. The only mystery about it was how it managed to keep running.

We set off one Sunday morning for the drive down south, rock music

22

blasting from the cassette deck, Alex had a box of his tapes on the back seat and he would pick one out at random, this one appeared to be a grunge mix-tape full of Nirvana, Soundgarden and Pearl Jam along with other bands I had never heard of but Alex knew them all and would tell me bits of information about each band that came on.

We arrived a little after an hour of driving, having stopped for snacks and cigarettes for Alex who only had the occasional smoke back then, usually only on a night out but he liked to have them with him.

The house itself was tucked away down a long overgrown path so we parked the car up and made our way into the woods at the side of the road. Alex had printed out directions from the website of how to find the house. After what seemed like hours we came to a clearing in the woods from where we could see the house.

It was clearly rundown and abandoned, the gardens surrounding it were overgrown and unkempt, all the glass in the windows had been smashed and replaced by wooden boards. Nevertheless it was an impressive building and must have been a grand mansion back in its heyday.

Alex and I fought our way through more undergrowth and eventually arrived at the entrance to the house. The door was blocked up but Alex said there was a window around the back that had been broken into and we could use it to enter the house, this turned out to be true and he squeezed through the gap in the wooden board and held it open for me as I climbed up and into the house. Inside the abandoned house it was dark and damp, Alex produced two huge torches from the backpack he had been carrying, he handed one to me and we flicked them on illuminating the large room.

In its day it must have been a grand ballroom, you could see the large ceiling roses where chandelier would have swung, a massive fireplace took up half one wall and the brickwork surrounding it was still impressive even in its dilapidated state.

We walked around the room for a while, Alex checking every nook and cranny for who knows what; after while he said we should go upstairs as that was where most people had had experiences.

The stairs, if you can call them that, were in a bad way, steps were missing, the hand rail had been completely broken off and I voiced my concern that it would not take our weight. Alex assured me it would be fine and we began our ascent, stepping carefully to avoid missing steps and the holes in the ones still there.

Arriving on the landing we scanned around with our torches and Alex began to make his way to what apparently had been the children's bedroom. Why is it always the kid's rooms that ghosts hang out it? I fully expected to see a pram or a cot rocking by itself when we entered the room, but of course anything like that had long since been looted.

The room was pretty much empty, a battered bed lay in one corner another fireplace took up part of the room; it seemed fireplaces were in nearly every room, I guess this place had not been updated to central heating. Alex shone his torch up the fireplace and squealed.

"What is it?" I had asked.

"I saw a squirrel scurry up the chimney!" Alex said with glee, I sighed and decided to look into the room next door. Leaving Alex to investigate this room on his own, he was too engrossed in the ancient floorboards to notice me leave.

In the next room it was much the same as before and I was slowly realizing this was not as exciting as Alex had made it seem; then I heard a voice and I stood frozen in spot.

It was barely audible; I listened intently but heard nothing more so put it down to imagination or the wind or something. Then as I began to walk around I heard it again, still feint but slightly more distinct this time and clearly a man's voice, no two men's voices.

"You have to take it" one voice whispered.

"You are the chosen one" the second voice said, they sounded eerily familiar.

I called out, thinking some kid had probably broken in like we had, but received no answer. I shivered and made my way back to the room Alex was in.

When I entered Alex was stood still, his skin white as snow and his eyes wide open, I asked him if he was okay and got no reply. I poked him in the ribs a few times and eventually he blinked and looked at me.

"What's up?" He asked, I explained he had zoned out and asked if he had heard any voices.

"Only yours" He laughed and whacked me on the back.

We explored the rest of the house, nothing else unusual happened and we left with Alex being disappointed that he hadn't experienced anything. I decided not to tell him about the voices as I began to doubt I heard them myself.

23

The following morning we all ate breakfast in the camper-van and consumed multiple cups of coffee, Alex was cleaning the dishes which was weird as he never seemed to do that at home.

"Feeling all right?" I asked him

"I'm just dandy mate, you?" He replied putting the last dish on the small draining board next to the campers sink.

"Feeling a little overwhelmed to be honest. It's all getting a bit much" I sighed.

"Yeah but what an adventure huh?" Alex was excited "The four of us saving the world from certain doom!"

"I'd rather there just wasn't any doom to begin with"

"Bah. Where's your sense of adventure? This is the best thing that's ever happened to us".

"That's not saying a lot" I laughed and Alex joined in. We went and sat with the others; I noticed Tarquin had curled himself up on Isabella's lap.

"Comfy Tarquin?" I asked smiling.

"Don't judge me, for some reason this human stroking my back has a soothing effect I cannot explain." He replied, a subtle purring noise coming from his body.

"It's 'cause you're a cat dude" Alex said, sitting down.

"Nonsense. I am not a cat!" Tarquin replied sulking. "I am a superior being from beyond your scope of understanding"

"Maybe so, but you still act like a cat" Alex laughed and attempted to pet Tarquin on the head; he hissed back at him then stopped embarrassed.

"Sorry, I don't know what came over me" he apologized.

"It's cool, cats don't usually like me anyway" Alex said.

"I am not a cat!" Tarquin yelled.

"Uh huh, whatever you say mister" Alex smiled and cracked open a can of Coke.

Calvin stood up to address us all "Perhaps we could return to the subject at hand? Namely the saving of life as we know it."

"Yes, we have no idea how much time we have before the planet is attacked" Tarquin nodded. "Are we all in agreement that we should return to my people so they can examine Jack fully?"

"There's not going to be any probing is there?" I asked.

"You wish!" Alex laughed.

"No probing, our systems are far more advanced than that. You will be placed in a machine which will scan your entire body, following that our scientists can evaluate the results and hopefully recreate your ability." Tarquin explained.

"OK, I guess" I said, unsure.

"The agreement is dependent on the conditions we set out last night yes?" Calvin asked.

"Yes, yes. I will take all four of you with me, as agreed." Tarquin said

"Great!" Said Alex "Can't wait!"

"How does it work? Can you beam us up?" I asked.

"Don't be stupid; teleportation is against the common laws of the physical world! We will need to return to the portal where we first encountered each other" Tarquin said.

"Well how does the portal work?" I asked

"It is far too complicated to explain to a human, suffice to say we will enter on your planet and arrive on mine".

Under his breath Alex said "Sounds a lot like teleportation to me".

"Will we be able to traverse the portal without time resetting or a loss of memory?" Calvin asked.

"You will with me at your side, don't worry I will not betray you." Tarquin reassured us.

"Very well, then I say we depart right away!" Calvin proceeded to the cabin and started the van's engine. Isabella joined him, sitting in the passenger seat.

"Could be our best adventure yet!" She said, holding Calvin's hand.

"Indeed my dear, truly out of this world" Calvin quipped; Isabella groaned and let go of his hand so he could drive the van.

After a short drive we arrived at the Duck and Goose, Calvin parked the camper in the pub car park and we all crept around the back. The pub wasn't open yet so we felt safe we would not be disturbed.

Standing in front of the shed Tarquin spoke up "Now remember, when we arrive all my race will appear in different forms in order not to melt your eyeballs"

"I've been meaning to ask" Isabella said "How come you are speaking English? And will the rest of your people speak the same?"

"I'm not speaking English; my race has developed so that whenever we speak it is translated to the person who hears its primary language. It's a common thing throughout the universes, your race has yet to evolve that far yet" Tarquin explained.

"That makes it easier" Isabella replied.

Tarquin continued "Now, in order for this to work you must all be joined with me. Isabella, if you would be so kind as to carry me in one arm and then all of you must hold hands with the person in front of you."

We did as instructed, Isabella in the front with Tarquin tucked under her arm, she reached behind her and held Calvin's hand who did the same with Alex. I was the last to go in and held onto Alex's hand.

"Ready mate?" He asked looking over his shoulder at me, the creepy doll was hanging out of his pocket and it gave me the thumbs up.

"As I'll ever be" I gulped.

"Then let us proceed" Said Tarquin and with that Isabella entered the tunnel and began to walk along it, the rest of us following close behind hands held tight.

"Ooh this is cool!" Said Alex, for him it was the first time again.

23

"Indeed, most interesting!" Said Calvin, as we walked on the familiar bright light started up again.

"Here we go goes, hope it works or we have to start this all over again!" I said.

"It will work" assured Tarquin.

The intensity of the light increased forcing us to close our eyes tight, it still felt bright even through my eyelids, then, suddenly it was dark again. Tentatively I opened one eye, then the other.

And that is how I ended up on a different planet.

24

"Holy crap we're in space!" Alex yelled.

"We are no more or less in space then when we left" Tarquin said.

"But...what about all the stars? And the sky is so dark?" Alex asked confused.

"It's night time." Tarquin replied deadpan.

"Idiot" I laughed jabbing Alex with my stump.

The planet we were on was beautiful. There were rolling fields of red grass, yes red, gorgeous huge trees towered over us, their leaves were varying shades of yellow and orange. Everything seemed so clean and the air smelt fresh and welcoming.

"This is amazing." I said "Have we arrived in the countryside?"

"No, this is the location of our main city, but to retain the natural beauty of the planet all buildings are underground." Tarquin explained. "I'll give you a moment to acclimatize then I will take you down.

The four of us walked around the area admiring the beauty of it all. The clear skies allowed the stars and moons (three moons that I could see) to illuminate the darkness. I came across a small pool of clear water, running my hand through the water I observed what I assumed were this planet's version of fish. They were square with fins and a tail the only features outside the cube shaped creatures; they swam gracefully through the clear water occasionally coming up to the surface to check out the new arrival to their world.

"Hey Tarquin" I called "Can these talk as well?"

24

"Of course not, who ever heard of a talking fish!" He laughed.

I stood up and wandered back to the group.

"Are we ready to continue?" Tarquin asked.

"Please. I am eager to experience more of this marvellous world." Calvin said, the rest of us nodded in agreement.

"Before we go on to the city I have a request." Tarquin said.

"You want the harness removed don't you?" Isabella asked.

"Yes. It is humiliating to wear and I see no further use for it now I have shown you what I can do"

"Of course" Isabella removed the harness and handed it to Calvin who tucked it into his jacket pocket.

"Thank you" Tarquin said "Now, please follow me".

We walked forward following Tarquin until we reached what I had assumed was a tree, on closer inspection it was made of some kind of metal and had a small door set within it. I reached out and put my hand on the metal, it felt natural, not like metal at all. It was warm to the touch similar to the walls of the tunnel in the shed, it felt like it was a living breathing material.

Tarquin scanned his paw over the side of the door and it slowly and silently opened.

"You may have to duck" Tarquin said to Calvin and beckoned us to enter.

"After you mate" Alex said to me.

"Gee thanks" I said and walked into the tree. Inside was roomier then it appeared from outside and I was soon joined by the others with Tarquin coming in last.

"Off we go" He said, swiping his paw on the wall by the door.

As the door closed behind us hundreds of small blue lights lit up the area, then I felt movement. It was barely detectable but you could just feel we were descending, so this was a lift.

"No elevator music?" Sniggered Alex. Tarquin just gave him a disapproving look.

A few seconds later the lift gently came to a stop and the doors opened up, Tarquin led us and we all followed him out into the main city.

You would never know we were underground; the sky appeared the same as it had on the surface and everything still had that fresh feeling in the air. This time however there were multiple buildings; all appeared to be made from the same metal as the tree lift. The buildings were different sizes but were all cubes, no rectangles or fancy architecture just simple cubes, each one coloured a slightly different shade to the next. One row was made of blue buildings and ranged from a very dark blue, almost black, to a colour that was nearing pure white with just a hint of its blue showing.

There were no roads, only smooth running streams of water, upon which several different sizes of what appeared to be boats silently made their way back and forth across the water. The boats too were made of this strange natural metal.

"What is this material your vessels and buildings are constructed with Tarquin?" Calvin asked.

"It is a natural substance that grows on this planet. It can be moulded and shaped into whatever you wish and it still retains its living state. It never rusts nor erodes and can be used forever, repurposing it into a different item if necessary."

"The ultimate recycling" I said.

"Indeed, unlike your planet we have an infinite amount of resources and have preserved the sanctity of our world for all time". Tarquin continued.

"Fascinating!" Calvin commented.

"Come, we will take a vessel to the science area. We must get Jack scanned so our people can start analysing the data." He motioned for us to follow him as he walked over to the waterway. A square boat immediately pulled up next to him and he jumped on board. The rest of us looked at each other, with a shrug Alex jumped on opposite Tarquin. The rest of us cautiously followed, expecting the boat to rock on the water. It did not, it remained perfectly stable and it felt like we could have still been on solid ground.

Once the last of us was on board the boat smoothly continued down the river, as we floated we saw more of the cubed buildings, a group of red ones with every red you could every think of incorporated. The same again with green buildings, then purple. In between each coloured block of buildings was luscious areas of red grassland, I could see what looked like people in the distance, they appeared to be dancing around a tree but it was hard to make out.

Another boat approached us and as it slowly passed I could see the sole inhabitant was a man but had a hand sticking out the top of his head, he also had three eyes. Tarquin waved a paw at the man and he waved back with the hand upon his head. The rest of us tried out best not to stare, except Alex who stood up and said "Whoa! Cool dude!" I tugged at his trousers to get him to sit down.

Soon the boat pulled over at a set of yellow buildings. I have no idea how the boat knew when to stop or where to go, it just seemed to do it automatically.

Tarquin leapt out and we all promptly followed, the boat staying motionless as we debarked.

"This is where our scientists work" Tarquin explained "Come, follow me" He started walking towards the yellow cubes.

"This is..." I started.

"Cool!" Said Alex.

"Fascinating" Said Calvin.

"Yeah, something like that." I continued.

"Tarquin, why do all your buildings appear to be cuboid in shape?" Calvin asked.

"A cube is simply the most practical shape to build in, we have no need for aesthetic architecture, preferring function over form. The colour differences are to mark the areas into designated zones, residential, commercial, medical etc.."

Calvin nodded satisfied with the answer.

We walked on in awe, as we approached one of the larger yellow cubes I noticed there were no doors or windows, Tarquin simply walked up to the building and a doorway opened seamlessly allowing him entry. We followed him inside and the door closed behind us leaving no indication it had ever been there.

We all looked around, taking it all in. The interior of the building was clearly clinical but still felt warm and welcoming with soft colour tones lining the walls of corridors that seemed to go on forever, each one smooth with no obvious doors.

In the centre of the room was a smaller cube, it was the only object in the room, Tarquin approached it and the top of the cube slid into itself. A woman appeared from within, rising up to greet us.

"Welcome all" She said, the words coming out from both of her two heads.

Alex whispered too me "Damn she's a hottie!"

"Dude, she has two heads?" I whispered back.

"Twice the beauty" He smiled and winked at me.

"Shush you two" Tarquin scowled "Give me a moment to explain to Lexa here what we need" He turned and began to converse with the woman in the cube desk.

"Anyone else a little freaked out?" I asked looking at the others.

"Nah it's great!" Said Alex

"I find it very interesting, a remarkable experience" Calvin said.

"It's certainly different" Said Isabella.

Tarquin finished his conversation and came over to us "This way" he stated and we followed him down one of the many corridors shooting off from the main room.

"Bye Lexa!" Alex waved at the receptionist, I cringed but she waved back.

We stopped partway down the corridor and a door appeared from nowhere, we all dutifully followed Tarquin into the room.

In stark conference to the previous quiet area this room was a hive of activity, machines were whirring, humming and beeping and people were running about flicking switches and turning dials. Mainly they appeared to be human-like each with differing deformities. One man had four arms, the extra two coming out from his chest and back. Another had the correct amount of limbs but his arms and legs were swapped over, he deftly walked along on his arms and used the machinery skilfully with his feet. It was remarkable to watch, and more than a little disturbing.

All the scientists appeared to be taking directions from a large owl that was sat in the centre of the room; it's back to us calling out orders. We followed Tarquin as he approached the owl.

"I have returned with the subject Doctor Hooter" He said, Alex and I sniggered to each other. Who chooses these names?

The owl's head rotated to look at us, it only had one eye but it was huge and took up the entire face of the creature. There was no room for a nose or mouth; how it spoke we had no idea.

"Ah Tarquin, good to see you old chap!" Hooter said from his invisible mouth "And this must be Jack and his friends, welcome one and all"

"A pleasure to make your acquaintance" said Calvin, slightly bowing.

"Hello" said Isabella.

"Hi" said Alex and I together.

"It is a pleasure to meet you all, I wish I had more time to converse with you all but we really must get our scans underway if we are to try and save your world." Hooter said motioning with his wing for one of the other scientists to come over. A short woman walked over, she appeared to be just limbs, no torso. Arms met legs in the middle.

"This is Tabitha, she is head of our science department" Hooter announced.

"Nice to meet you all, Jack if you would come with me we can get the scan over with and then you can all relax whilst we analyse the results." Tabitha said, and then to Tarquin she said "Have all the subjects passed the initial health scan?"

"What health scan?" I asked.

"All beings are scanned when they go through the portal for any current illnesses or diseases, the scanner then carries out any medical attention it deems necessary" Tarquin explained.

"We were only in the portal for mere moments, your technology is able to fully scan and administer medical treatment in such a short time?" Calvin asked.

"Of course, as it happens two of you required no treatment". Tarquin continued

"Wait, so two of us did? What did you do to us?" Alex asked.

"Well Alex, you should find that rash is all healed up" Tarquin started, Alex looked sheepish "And Isabella you will find you no longer have cancer".

Isabella stood eyes wide and mouth agape.

"Really?" asked Calvin.

"Yes" smiled Tarquin "It has all been eradicated and Isabella is back to full health"

Isabella finally spoke "That's... that's.... amazing! Thank you so much" tears rolled down her cheeks as she hugged Calvin close. Alex joined in for a hug as I was led away by Tabitha.

"Your race is clearly far more advanced than mine" I said.

"Well of course, our race is one of the most advanced in the universe, yours is...er...somewhere lower" she looked away from me "Anyway this here is the scanning machine, it is more advanced than the one you came through to get here so will take a little longer."

The machine looked simply enough, a glass tube with room for a person to stand in.

"OK, what do I have to do?" I asked.

"Just climb inside, lay back and we will do the rest" Tabitha said "I would recommend you change into our clothing to avoid getting yours wet"

"Wet? What sort of scanner is this?"

"It uses fluid to fully encapsulate the body, the fluid contains millions of nanobots which will scan every inch of you" she explained.

"I see." I said, I didn't see at all.

"Here take these and change into them in that room there" she pointed to a blank wall.

I took the clothes she handed me, it was basically a grey boiler suit, it looked like it was far too big for me but I wasn't about to ask if they had it in my size. I took the suit and walked over to the wall that Tabitha had pointed at looking for a door.

"Um..." I uttered.

"Walk nearer" Tabitha replied, already adjusting settings on the scanning machine. I walked forward and from nowhere a door opened in the wall, stepping inside lights came on and I saw it was a small room with lockers and a bench. The door closed behind me and I changed into the gigantic suit, as soon as the suit was on it immediately shrunk down to perfectly fit my form. Impressed I walked back to where I had come in and the door opened for me again.

24

"How do I look?" I asked.

"Does it matter?" Tabitha replied not looking up from the machine "It's for practicality not fashion".

"Fair enough" I sighed "Now what?"

"Hop in and we will get started" Tabitha waved her hand over a panel and the glass tube slid smoothly upwards. I hesitantly stepped inside and stood, the machine slowly began to tilt backwards and I found myself lying against the back wall, not entirely flat but close to it.

"Ready?" Asked Tabitha.

"I guess so" I replied.

The glass tube began to descend again encapsulating me inside it; from the angle I was at I couldn't see what Tabitha was doing so I just looked up at the ceiling.

"Next is the nanobot fluid" Tabitha said and I began to feel wetness at my feet, the liquid continued to rise upwards covering my leg, then my chest before reaching my neck. It was at this point I realized the water was not stopping.

"Um...Tabitha? Humans can't breathe under water!" I panicked.

"Neither can we, it's not water" Tabitha calmly replied.

"What..." I tried to speak but the water had reached my mouth so instead I held my breath as it continued to flow up over my nose and eventually covered my entire body head to toe. A few moments passed and I was struggling, I thrashed inside the tube but I was pinned tight by the machine. Eventually I gasped releasing the air I had held fully expecting to drown on this alien planet. But then I discovered that I could breathe perfectly normally, the sensation was unreal. I laughed in relief, bubbles flowing from my mouth. The water began to subside and once my mouth was free I yelled

"That was wild" I was still laughing.

"Glad you liked it" Tabitha said emotionlessly "Stay where you are and the machine will dry you"

I did as instructed and sure enough once all the fluid had drained away heat blasted out through the tube and in seconds I was bone dry again. The tube tilted back to an upright position and slid open once more.

"All done, come on out" Tabitha said.

I stepped out of the machine and looked myself over, "What next?" I asked.

"That's it for you" Tabitha stated "We will now need to analyse the results; you can go and join your friends now."

"Can I keep the suit?" I asked grinning.

"I suppose so, you humans are an odd species" She shook her head and motioned for me to leave. As I started to walk away she stopped me.

"One more thing" she said and opened up a drawer in a nearby unit, from it she produced a box about the size of a shoe box, she opened the box and there, sat on a luxurious red pillow, was my left hand.

"Oh my god! Thank you!" I said taking the hand. I looked it over and held it up to my stump where my ability did its thing and it finally was back in place. I wiggled my fingers and grinned, the hand was in perfect condition.

"You're welcome" said Tabitha "Sorry we stole it from you, we had no idea you would be an ally, now go, join your friends". She waved me away and I walked over to the other three who were deep in conversation with Hooter and Tarquin.

"Hey, hey, looks whose back! And with some fancy new duds I see" Alex smiled.

"Yep, just call me a dedicated follower of fashion!" I replied "And look!" I waved my left hand at them all, a muted cheer went up from the three of them.

"Glad you are well my friend. Doctor Hooter here has suggested we get a bite to eat whilst they study the results of your scan. Are you hungry?" Calvin asked.

"I could eat" I said.

25

When I turned 18 Alex made a big deal about going to the pub together, I had been sneaking drinks for a couple of years but now that I was legal he insisted we go to his favourite hangout the Duck and Goose.

Armed with my new provisional learner's license (I hadn't yet passed my test but I was taking lessons and getting better all the time) I thanked my parents for the presents they had gifted me and headed off to meet Alex.

The Duck and Goose was your usual town pub, slightly run down but with a good mix of locals and passers-by, it didn't do meals but you could get a pork pie or a packet of pork scratchings if you got peckish. Alex marched up to the bar and placed and called out to the landlord.

"Tom! A pint of bitter and whatever my young friend here wants" He called, patting me hard on the back. The landlord politely informed him that his name was Bill, not tom. Alex waved this off dismissively and turned to me; I ordered a lager, I wasn't yet into drinking bitter or anything heavier but Alex insisted we also had some tequila shots to celebrate the big day and who was I to turn it down?

We sat in a booth and consumed multiple drinks as the night progressed, various people came to wish me happy birthday, I had no idea who they all were but Alex seemed to know everyone. Many shots and pints were bought for me and by time last orders were called I was swimming inside my own head. Standing up I swayed from side to side, Alex laughed but helped steady me and insisted on walking me home.

Halfway home I announced I needed to sit down so we stumbled into a park and found a bench to rest on, it was summer and the nights were warm, that plus the alcohol made me relaxed. It was then I thought it time to tell Alex about my ability.

He of course did not believe me at first so I took my left shoe and sock off and proceeded to detach my foot and wave it in his face.

"Jesus!" he yelled mesmerized by the foot, I put it back on and off several times then did the same with my left hand.

"That's bloody bonkers mate!" He said with a huge grin on his face.

I regaled the tale of what had happened to me in those formative years, and made him swear his silence; he made a motion as if zipping his mouth shut.

The next day I thought I would have regrets about revealing my secret, thinking Alex might view me differently but apart from my first proper hangover nothing changed, we were still as close as before, maybe even closer.

The alcohol had made it easier to spill my secret to Alex but I realized it was more than that, here was someone who got me and didn't judge, he just took it all in his stride. I never had many friends after leaving the facility and Alex was always there for me, he may have been an idiot but he would stand by my side no matter what.

26

The alien canteen was huge with multiple tables and chairs lining the space, all made of the same metal as the buildings. The room looked all the bigger because we were the only people in it.

"Why is it so quiet?" I asked Tarquin,

"Most people are asleep right now. Only the department dedicated to studying you is still working. It also helps that people who have not changed forms have been told to stay away whilst you are here, lest you be exposed to our true visages" He replied.

"Makes sense" Alex said "So what do we get to eat?"

"Anything you like" Tarquin started "This canteen can provide any food from any world in any universe as long as we have visited it at least once."

"Anything?" Alex smiled.

"Try it, just say what you want out loud" Tarquin answered.

"OK, I'll have the dish of the day from Jupiter please!" Alex said loudly.

"There is no life on Jupiter, thus no food" Tarquin rolled his eyes.

"Ah damn, was hoping for something weird" Alex looked disheartened.

Isabella spoke up "Can I just have a roast beef dinner please?" she asked. Instantly a machine appeared from out of the wall, it smoothly hovered over to our table and placed a covered plate in front of Isabella. She lifted the lid and underneath was the most perfectly made roast beef, roast potatoes, Yorkshire pudding and all the trimmings. The food robot then placed a large steaming jug of gravy next to her.

"Wow!" Isabella gasped "This is perfect!" She picked up the gravy jug and proceeded to drown everything in thick brown liquid.

"Can never have too much gravy!" She winked at Calvin and started to tuck in to her meal.

Calvin laughed and requested the same meal, I decided to keep it simple and asked for a big mac and fries with a banana milkshake. Both meals promptly arrived and we began to eat. Alex was the only one without a meal.

"Still can't decide?" I asked him.

"It's difficult; a choice of everything is too much choice!" He replied "OK, I think I've got it! Bring be the most unusual dish in all the universes! Oh as long as it is safe for human consumption" He added.

The robot appeared once again, this time with a huge covered platter, it placed it in front of Alex who was grinning like a child at Christmas. He lifted the lid of the platter and underneath was a writhing mix of blue tentacles, small yellow shell like things and a bunch of other stuff I can't even describe. I looked at Alex.

"Tuck in mate" I laughed.

Alex looked at the plate of food for a minute, then, picking up a knife and fork, he proceeded to take a bite of the meal. The rest of us stared, waiting for his reaction. After a few chews he swallowed and said

"Delicious!" We all looked shocked as he began to chuck more of the moist mess into his mouth. "What?" He said with a mouthful of some kind of green noodles "It's surprisingly good!"

I shrugged my shoulders and continued eating my burger. We sat in silence as we ate, Tarquin tucked into a bowl of cat food, telling us he had acquired a taste for it during his time on earth. Whilst the rest of us finished our meal only Alex still had food left to eat. He forked a few more morsels into his mouth and then sat back pushing the plate away.

"I'm done" he said "I can't eat another bite" he rubbed his stomach satisfyingly.

"I trust everything was to your liking?" Tarquin asked, we all agreed the food was excellent; Alex just gave two thumbs up. "Good, good. If you are ready I will show you to your rooms where you can freshen up and get some rest if you like."

"Sounds good to me" Alex said "I'm ready for a nap!"

26

"I would be curious to explore more of your world" Calvin said.

"I'm afraid you will not be able to leave this building, you must understand that if you should come across one of my species in our true form it will not be good for you" Tarquin said sadly.

"Of course, I remember when we saw your true from and have no wish to repeat that experience. I will be satisfied with seeing the sleeping quarters" Calvin nodded.

"Very well, if you will all follow me" Calvin stood up and stretched his six legs out. The rest of us stood and followed him to the wall, which of course opened up in front of him, we were about to step through when Isabella spoke up.

"What about our plates? Shouldn't we help to clear up" She asked.

"Don't worry about that, the machines will take care of everything. See?" He said pointing a paw back where we had been sat. The table was totally cleared and looked as though we had never been there at all. There was no sign of the robots anywhere; I assumed they had disappeared back into the wall.

"Impressive!" Said Isabella, turning to Calvin she said "We could do with them at home."

Calvin laughed "Indeed that would be most useful!" We walked on down the blank corridor, taking a few turns here and there before Tarquin stopped.

"Here we are, Isabella and Calvin this is your room" He said motioning to a blank wall which opened up into a door as he approached it.

"Thank you Tarquin, for everything" Isabella bent down and stroked Tarquin's head, he began to purr. She and Calvin went through the open doorway and it slowly closed behind them.

"You are in here Alex, and Jack your room is opposite" Tarquin pointed and Alex walked towards the wall and through the door that appeared.

"See you later mate" he said disappearing into the room, when he was gone Tarquin turned to me.

"I see he still has the doll, that's a good sign." He said.

"If you say so, still creeps me out though" I replied.

"Just wait, once it has made its decision you will be blessed with a new power, which may help us in the coming days"

"Or it may be another useless power like I already have" I said, not convinced.

"Your power may be what saves your planet, not so useless after all" Tarquin smiled and began to walk away "Rest well Jack, I will come get you all when the time is right"

I walked into my room feeling tired, the light came on automatically as I entered and illuminated the room in a soft glow.

27

I slumped down in a comfy bean bag like chair and took in my surroundings. The room was basic but cosy; the walls, despite being made of the weird natural metal, gave off a warm feeling. Furniture comprised of a large bed, a desk with matching chair, a bedside cabinet and the large chair I was currently occupying. It had clearly been fitted out for human use and I wondered if we were the first people to have come to this planet.

Feeling exhausted I decided to lay down on the bed, I checked my phone and saw it only had five percent battery left so I switched it off and put in on the bedside table, immediately it buzzed and the battery icon lit up indicating it was charging somehow. I'd say I was amazed but after everything I'd experienced over the last few days a wireless charging cabinet was the least of it all. Before I laid down I looked around for a light switch, finding nothing of the sort I thought "screw it" and collapsed on to the bed, at which points the lights naturally dimmed to a low glow "Well there you go" I muttered before closing my eyes.

After a while trying to nap it became obvious I was too wired for sleep, my mind reeling over all that had happened. I sat up and the lights increased again, picking up my phone I saw it had full charge so I turned it back on. I was not surprised to see I had no signal; the nearest cell tower being god knows how many light years away in another universe. I contemplated waking Alex to see if he was awake, then thought better of it; if he could sleep I should let him. Instead I decided to do a little exploring, I walked up to where I had entered the room and the wall opened up for me.

The corridor outside my room was quiet; it occurred to me that it would impossible to find my room again, there were no indications or door numbers anywhere to be seen. I went back in the room and rummaged through the desk, inside was a small notepad and pen, I took them and wrote "my room" on it, pocketing the pad and pen I went back outside and I held the page up against the door jamb so as it closed it trapped the piece of paper in place. "Good enough" I whispered and crept down the hall.

I decided to follow my video game logic of always heading left, that way it should be easier to find my way back but just to be sure on each corner I left a page with an arrow on it pointing back the way I had come. I just had to hope the pages would stay in place.

I walked in the centre of the corridor in case I should trigger one of the invisible doors and wake someone up, I had no idea if anyone else was here but wasn't about to take the chance of pissing off a sleeping alien. After a couple of left turns I was out of the corridors and into a wide open space, it appeared to be a nature room with trees, plants and even a small stream running through it with little bridges crossing it here and there. It wasn't exactly my woods but it was peaceful nonetheless.

Of course everything was made of metal but it all seemed so natural and alive. I crossed one of the bridges and sat on a bench overlooking the stream, I could see the square fish I had observed before swimming to and fro. The whole place was extremely calm and relaxing and I felt my eyes getting droopy.

Just then I heard footsteps and my eyes shot open, before I had a chance to find somewhere to hide Lexa, the two-headed receptionist we had met earlier, came around the corner and spotted me.

"Oh" she said, the words coming out of both mouths "I didn't realize anyone was in here."

"I'm sorry" I started "I know I was supposed to stay in my room but I was so restless."

"It's okay, I like to come here too to relax, it's very soothing" She talked over to me and motioned to the bench I was sat on, "May I?"

"Oh, of course" I shuffled over to make room and she sat down next to me. For a moment there was an awkward silence, then she spoke up.

27

"You know you and your friends are the first humans I have met" It was like listening to something in stereo.

"Really? So no others of my kind have been here before?" I asked

"Nope, you are the first" She replied.

"Well then I am honoured" I said.

"As you should be" she laughed "We don't normally let outsiders onto our planet. You must be very important on your world"

This time I laughed "No not at all! I can just do something no other human can do, it's never been any help to me but Tarquin seems to think I can help you guys"

"Interesting, I have heard of your ability, tell me does the one you call Alex have any special powers?" both her faces actually blushed when she said this.

"Alex? No, he's just a regular human. Well, he's special in his own way" I said.

"Oh? How so?" Lexa asked.

"Well nothing fazes him, he just adapts to whatever the situation is and he's always willing to try anything" I explained.

"Sounds like an interesting person" Lexa smiled a little.

"I guess he is, he's my best friend and has always been there for me, good times and bad" I was reminiscing the times Alex had managed to get me out of depressive slumps. "I guess his ability was to turn any situation into a positive, I'm lucky to have him as a friend."

"That's good to hear" she said and we both settled back into silence for a moment.

After a while I could feel my eyes getting heavy again and decided I ought to go back to my room.

"I'll walk with you" Lexa said standing "There's really not much else to see here, just this relaxation area, the science labs and the living quarters."

The two of us made our way through the corridors, Lexa noticed the pieces of paper on the floor, she picked one of them up and examined it.

"Ah, that was me" I said "I figured I needed a way to find my room again" Lexa laughed "So you are a smart one!" She said

"I wouldn't go that far" I joined in laughing with her "just how do you find your way around here? None of the doors are visible until you approach them so it all looks the same."

"I've never really thought about it before, it's just something we can do without thinking" She shrugged her shoulders and we walked on until we reached the page from the notepad I had left, it looked like it was just growing out of the wall.

"This is me" I said awkwardly, I approached the door and it opened for me.

"Rest well Jack, I am glad to have met you and hope we can talk more in the future" Lexa extended a hand, I shook it, deciding not to try my usual trick on her.

"It's been a stressful experience so it's nice to just chat with someone"

"Even someone with two heads?" She smirked.

I laughed "Yes, even someone with two heads" I went back into my room and gave Lexa a wave as the door shut, she waved back. Feeling this time sleep would be forthcoming I once more climbed into the bed and was asleep within minutes.

28

It was on one of Alex and my many trips to the pub that I met Anne, she was a friend of a friend of Alex and came over to say hello to him, Alex introduced us and I was immediately smitten.

She was a student, a year older than me and was what people like to call an 'alternative' girl; green hair, nose and lip piercings and always wore funky gothic clothing. I don't know if that was my 'type' but whatever it was Anne pulled the look off flawlessly. She was beautiful and I couldn't take my eyes off her.

She sat with us for a while and despite my anxiousness I found her easy to chat with her about anything and everything but mostly movies and music. It wasn't until two hours had passed that I realized it was just the two of us in the booth, Alex and his other friends were over by the bar.

I was inexperienced in the ways of dating but Anne was no shrinking violet and when it came time to leave she insisted I walk her home. Alex gave me a knowing wink and said he would see me tomorrow.

On the walk home we chatted some more before she grabbed me, pinned me up against a nearby wall and started to kiss me. Inexperienced or not I fully kissed her back, after a few minutes of making out she pulled away, a huge grin on her face.

"I thought I better make the first move as it didn't look like you would!" She laughed.

I blushed and said nothing; we spent the rest of the walk hand in hand (no I didn't pop my hand off!) before arriving at her student house. Once there she asked me if she could meet me tomorrow for lunch, my head nearly fell off from nodding yes, she laughed and we kissed again for some time before finally separating.

I walked the rest of the way home in a kind of euphoric state, not quite believing what had happened to me. That night I slept well dreaming of that first kiss and the green haired girl who had stolen my heart in just one night.

The following day we met up as agreed at a local café that catered mainly to students, we talked, we laughed and we couldn't keep our hands and eyes off of each other. I barely touched the food in front of me and eventually Anne asked if I was done, I said I was and she grabbed my hand and stood up.

"Come on" she said "my housemates are all out today" with this she led me out of the café and into her car where we kissed for a while before she drove us back to her place.

29

When I woke up I thought I was back in my own bed and groaned at the prospect of having time slipped again, as my brain caught up with my body I realized I was still in the alien bedroom. I could hear a gentle rapping at my door so I walked across the room so the door opened for me. Tarquin was stood outside.

"Morning Jack" he said "I see you are dressed" I didn't mention I had never got undressed in the first place.

"Morning Tarquin, is everything okay?" I asked

"Yes, just wanted to see if you wanted breakfast?" He asked.

The mentioning of eating woke my stomach up and it growled loudly.

"Sounds like you do" Tarquin laughed "Would you mind getting Alex up and I'll go and get Isabella and Calvin."

"Sure, no problem...um...where is his door again?" I asked looking at the blank walls.

Tarquin sighed and pointed a paw at a place on the wall opposite my room, he then wandered further up the corridor to the others room. I walked up to where he had pointed and stood as close to the wall as I could. Nothing happened so I knocked on the wall.

"Alex?" I called "You up?" a little louder, I heard a muffled voice from behind the wall. I waited a few moments then tried again, this time the door opened just as I was knocking on it. Standing there was Lexa looking dishevelled and embarrassed.

"Um....Hi Jack...I was just..." She muttered

"Hi Lexa, no need to explain" I smiled at her; she gave a shy grin back and turned her heads back into the room.

"Will I see you later Alex?" She asked.

"Of course!" Alex's voice came from within the room. Lexa walked out of the room, her heads looking at the floor as she went passed me and down the corridor. I walked into Alex's room to find him pulling on a t-shirt.

"You sly dog" I said grinning.

"I think I'm in love!" Alex was positively glowing.

"After one night?" I asked.

"One amazing night!" He replied "I'm starving, is there anything to eat?" He swiftly changed the subject.

"Yeah, Tarquin and the others are waiting for us so we can go eat" I replied motioning towards the corridor.

"Then let us eat!" He said and followed me out the room, further down the corridor we met up with Isabella and Calvin.

"Morning guys" I said.

"Good morning my young friends, how did you sleep?" Calvin asked, I looked at Alex who just jabbed me in the arm.

"Not bad" I said, Alex just grinned.

"Tarquin has gone ahead, he gave us instructions on how to find the canteen" Isabella said.

"Then lead on, breakfast awaits us!" Alex said. The four of us made our way down the winding corridor, stopping every so often for Isabella to remember which way to go. Eventually we arrived at the familiar room where we had eaten last night.

Inside Tarquin was waiting for us along with Tabitha the doctor, we all exchanged pleasantries as we sat down. The food robot appeared and we all placed out orders in turn. Alex and I went with a full English breakfast, Calvin opted for porridge and Isabella went with a fruit salad. Tabitha had ordered something but we had no idea what it was, she seemed to be enjoying it. Tarquin had a whole raw salmon and greedily tucked into it, finished before the rest of us.

Once the last of us was done eating I asked Tabitha how the research was coming.

"Your body is amazing " She said "Scientifically speaking" she added quickly.

"So will it work? Copying his ability?" Isabella asked.

"That we have not been able to repeat as of yet, the things you can do with your body is a scientific mystery. I knew you could remove arms and legs but there is so much more you can do" Tabitha continued.

"Really? I've never found much use for my power" I said.

"I don't think you realize the full potential your ability gives you, did you know you can remove any body part? Not just limbs."

Alex laughed "Oh god, don't tell me our next adventure will be looking for his penis!" I poked him in the ribs.

Tabitha was unfazed "Well yes he could do that, but also he could detach a toe, a finger his nose, and ear, possibly even his whole head and still retain mentally intact"

"I don't fancy trying that!" I said shocked "How would I reattach it without the use of my body."

"That's the other thing, according to my findings you should be able to still control any part of your body after it has become detached" Tabitha explained.

I sat back in my chair stumped.

"That would be awesome!" Said Alex

"It would be most useful" added Calvin.

"I guess…" I started "But it's not something I've ever been able to do before" I continued.

"Perhaps we need further research, but as far as I can surmise the only thing stopping you from being able to do it is a mental block, not a physical one." Tabitha said.

"He's always had a bit of a mental block when it comes to believing in himself" Alex said, I glared at him but said nothing because I knew he was right. I had always had low self-esteem, never believing I would amount to anything so never really trying. I blamed it on the years I spent in the government institution stunting my emotional progress but to be honest that excuse was getting a little old. The silence in the room was interrupted by

Doctor Hooter flying into the room; he appeared to be in a panic as he flapped around eventually landing on the back of a chair.

"We have a problem!" He panted.

"What's happened? Are we too late?" Tarquin asked.

"It seems so" Hooter replied sadly.

"Too late for what?" I asked.

"I am sorry to be the bearer of bad news but it seems the enemy has arrived on your planet and we have not yet perfected human mimicry" The owl explained.

"The X-Borgs are on earth?!" Alex yelled standing up.

"The what?" Hooter looked at Tarquin who waved a paw dismissively

"It's what they have named them, given they couldn't pronounce their real name I let it go." He explained.

"Fair enough" Hooter nodded "Well then yes, the…X-Borgs have arrived on earth, well at least some of them"

"Some of them?" Calvin queried "How many?"

"It appears to just be a scouting party at this stage, we believe it is a small group, no more than three or four of them." Hooter continued.

"Only four? We can take them!" Alex yelled defiantly.

"What?!" Tarquin and I both said together.

"Well, you need humans to infiltrate them right? We are humans, as normal looking as they come, we could do it." Alex was relishing the idea.

"I don't think that's wise" Tarquin said "You have not had the training, it would be suicide" he shook his head.

"I have to agree with Tarquin, it does not sound like a viable option" Calvin said.

"If you guys are right then we are dead anyway, at least this way we have a chance." Alex pleaded

Tarquin and Hooter looked at each other for a minute before Hooter spoke

"I suppose he has a point"

"Does he though?" I said.

"Your species is doomed if we can't stop the invasion before it starts, you'd be dead or captured anyway so may as well go down fighting. But we can't

29

ask you to do this; it must be your decision." Hooter continued.

"What do you think Jack? Fancy saving the world?" Alex beamed.

"Not really, but you know me, I'll follow your lead" I shrugged my shoulders.

"That means he's in! What about you guys?" He turned towards Calvin and Isabella.

Calvin was about to answer when Tarquin spoke up.

"If you are going to do this then it would be best it just the two of you. Fewer people would make it easier to get captured, plus I fear Calvin's stature would make him seem like a threat and therefore more likely to be killed than captured" He said.

"Fair enough, good points. I guess it's you and me then Jack!" Alex smiled.

"We will endeavour to help in any way we can" Calvin said, Isabella nodded in agreement.

"Then it's decided. Jack and I will get caught and sabotage the X-Borgs from within while Team B" Alex motioned to the others in the room "Will monitor things from the outside, do you have those little things that spies wear in their ears to talk to each other?"

"We can certainly provide you with that, and any technology we have" Hooter replied.

"Okay then! Let's start planning, to the war room!" Alex yelled raising his hand in the air.

Tarquin and Hooter looked at each other.

"War room?" Queried Hooter.

"Yeah, you know, where we plan our mission and stuff? You guys don't have a war room?" Alex looked disappointed.

"No Alex, we do not have a 'war room'" Tarquin rolled his eyes.

"Oh, well I guess any room will do" Alex said deflated.

"Why don't we go to my lab, there we can see maps of your planet and find out where the X-Borgs are headed." Hooter said.

"Excellent!" Then to the War Lab!" Alex began to march off, the rest of us shrugged and stood up to follow him.

"Um...which way?" He said, stopping.

Tarquin sighed "Follow me" he said and stepped out into the hallway.

30

Hooter's lab was next door to the science room where I had been scanned by the nanobots, it was a smaller area but afforded plenty of space for the six of us to gather around a large desk.

Holographic maps of earth rose up from unseen projectors and Hooter could easily manipulate them with a wave of one of his wings. From what we could tell the X-Borg recon party was using London as their base of operations, they were keeping out of site in a warehouse district where few members of the public would go. Several of those that worked in the area had already been captured by the aliens and were being kept in one of the warehouses.

"Your job" Tarquin began "Will be to enter this area as if you worked there, undoubtedly the X-Borgs will want to stop anyone leaving the area and will take you hostage"

"Sounds good Captain." Alex said nodding.

"I'm not a Captain" Tarquin replied.

"Oh, OK, what rank do you hold then?" Alex asked.

"We don't have ranks on this planet, we are all equal" Hooter explained.

"Well that's very woke of you!" Alex said.

"If you say so" Tarquin said "Now our only concern is the X-Borgs already have enough prisoners and decide to vaporize you on the spot."

"That is definitely a concern!" I said.

"Nah, we'll be good mate. We will make perfect prisoners" Alex patted me on the back.

"If you say so" I sighed.

"Once you are in, and not dead, we will communicate with you from outside the area, using these communicators" Hooter waved his wing over a cabinet and it opened up to reveal several small black squares.

"Cool!" Said Alex "What about guns?"

"Guns will get you killed straight away" Tarquin explained.

"Oh, well that's not good" Alex said.

"No it would be rather counterproductive. Besides we don't need you to fight them, we just need you to get our technology into theirs. This will infect their systems with a virus which will be sent unknown to their mother ship causing it to fail and have to return to their own planet." Hooter detailed.

"What about the ones already here?" I asked.

"We will have to deal with them in a more...physical way" Tarquin said.

"Shoot 'em all!" Alex yelled.

"Something like that" Tarquin sighed "But that is after we have injected the virus into their system, without that any action is pointless"

"Once they have returned to their home planet what is to stop them from returning to Earth to attempt a takeover once more?" Calvin asked.

"It has taken them hundreds of years travelling the universes to get to your planet, even if they do attempt to return we will have plenty of time to prepare." Tarquin explained.

"We'll be ready!" Alex said.

"We'll be long dead Alex" I said.

"Oh yeah, good point, well our great, great, grand-kids can deal with it."

"That's if we survive this plan" I said

"We can do it mate, I have complete faith in us!" Alex said.

"Glad someone does" Tarquin muttered under his breath, Alex either didn't hear or chose to ignore the comment.

We continued to go through the plan; Hooter showed us how to work the equipment we would have access to. Alex and I would just be wearing the earpieces; the rest of the equipment would go with Tarquin, Calvin and Isabella. Hooter would remain here; it being decided his owl form not being particularly helpful on earth.

Once all the details were confirmed Alex spoke up.

"Just one more thing" He said "Can I get one of those jumpsuits like Jack?

They are kind of cool and if we were matching we would look more like workers at the warehouses."

Tarquin and Hooter looked at each other "I don't see why not" Tarquin said.

"Thanks, also, I need to go say goodbye to Lexa before we leave"

"Lexa? What for?" Hooter asked.

"Alex has a girlfriend" I jokingly sang.

"Oh good grief" Tarquin rolled his eyes once more "Go on then, I'll get everything organized and we meet back here in one hour. Time is of the essence."

"No problem boss!" Alex said and shot out of the lab.

"Bless him" said Isabella once he had left.

"He always did go for the weird girls, two heads is a new one though" I said.

"I'm more concerned they are different species! Hooter said.

"When in Rome, I suppose" Said Calvin.

"We're all doomed" signed Tarquin.

31

An hour later we gathered once more in Doctor Hooters lab, Alex was now dressed in a jumpsuit the same as mine. We did look like a pair who worked together so Alex's idea surprisingly made sense. Lexa was at his side and they were holding hands and kept looking at each other, I had no idea how Alex decided which face to look at.

"We just realized something!" Alex said "Lexa and Alex are anagrams of each other!"

"Well it must be fate then" I smiled.

"Yep!" He replied, putting his arm around Lexa.

"Yes, well. Are we all ready?" Hooter asked, we all nodded in reply. "Good, then let us proceed to the portal."

Using the same lift as before we arrived back on the surface of the planet, it was daylight now and the bright glare of the sun made everything look different.

"Wasn't the grass red before?" I asked Tarquin.

"That's correct, red at night, blue during the day, totally normal for this planet" he replied.

We made our way back to the portal we had used to first enter this planet; it seemed like a lifetime ago. As we made our way Tarquin explained some things to us.

"As agreed, Calvin will use his van to take the five of us into London where we can park up as a base of operations. We have portals all over the world but the one in your town is the nearest to where we need to be. Lexa, I'm afraid you will not be able to join us, you are simply too conspicuous".

"Of course, I understand" she said, turning to Alex "I will miss you my love" She kissed him on the cheek.

"I'll be back gorgeous" He replied and planted a kiss on her lips, then did the same with her other head.

"Let us hope our friends make it through this unscathed" Calvin said.

Isabella turned to Doctor Hooter "I want to thank you again for what you did for me, I can never repay you. You have given me my life back and I am eternally grateful."

"It is our pleasure my dear" Hooter bowed, as much as an owl can bow "We have spent many years perfecting our medical facility and I'm glad to know it works on humans"

"So you didn't know it would work?" I asked, concerned.

"Oh no, we had no idea what the effects of our health scan would have on your species, it could just have easily have turned your bodies inside out, what a mess that would have been!" Hooter laughed while the rest of us stood staring in shock, he suddenly realized what he had said and tried to backtrack "Um...of course that was a very unlikely scenario! We are highly skilled scientists after all."

"Uh huh" I muttered.

"Ah well, it all worked out didn't it!" Alex said gazing at Lexa, she smiled at him and I began to think he really had fallen in love this time and not just one of his one night stands.

"Are we ready to proceed?" Calvin asked.

"Let's do it!" Said Alex geared up and ready for adventure, I was less excited by the prospect of purposely getting captured by an alien race hell-bent on destruction but I agreed nevertheless.

Tarquin waved his paw in the air and a doorway appeared revealing the familiar long metal corridor that had started this whole adventure. Isabella opened her arms and he leapt into them, we mimicked what he had done before with all of us holding hands forming a chain as Isabella stepping into the doorway, Tarquin tucked cosily under one arm.

We all knew what to expect this time but the flash of light still took us by surprise, within seconds it was over and we were stood on the patio at the back of the Duck and Goose. A very startled landlord stood there clasping several pint glasses which promptly fell to the floor smashing into a thousand pieces.

"What the fuck?" He said.

32

After meeting Anne the two of us were inseparable, any free time we had was spent together. Her parents had died in an accident when she was a child and she had been shuffled from one foster family to another until she turned 18 and was kicked out of the system, she managed to get a room in a shared house and we would mainly hang out their together.

When college came to an end we both applied and got accepted at the same university, we had our own rooms in different halls but most of the time I slept in her room, it being the nicer of the two, plus mine had a weird smell that just wouldn't go away.

University was only an hour by train back home so we would often go back and visit Alex who had decided uni wasn't for him, he was busy hosting websites, the money wasn't great but it made him happy and meant he could spend most of his time online, he never seemed to run out of things to research.

One night in Anne's room we had been out drinking and were chilling in front of the TV, I had been agonizing about telling Anne my secret and ultimately decided she needed to know the whole me.

She took it remarkably well, a little freaked out at first but soon fascination over took fear and she was asking me question after question about what I could do. I answered all her questions as best I could, and she got me to take off a hand or foot. She actually seemed to think it was pretty cool, I was ecstatic that I had not scared her away.

That first year of university was bliss, I was enjoying my course and both Anne and I were doing well with our studies despite spending all our free time drinking and having fun together. Anne wasn't a big party person, which suited me fine, and although we had a few friends we would drink with it was generally just the two of us watching stupid comedies in her dorm room whilst sharing a huge bottle of vodka.

We would often half joke about getting married and what our wedding would be like, who we would invite (only essential friends and family), what music we would play (Anne insisted on punk rock) and what we would serve for food (I insisted on burgers and root beer). Looking back I think I was ready to propose but was terrified of rejection so I never plucked up the courage to ask, we were still young anyway and I thought we had all the time in the world.

It was the best time of my life; I finally had a best friend and a girlfriend I loved. Of course life has a way of shitting on you when you are at your highest.

33

We were all inside the Duck And Goose, Calvin was attempting to reassure the landlord that it was just some elaborate prank we had pulled appearing out of his shed late at night. The pub had closed for the evening and Bill the landlord was luckily alone, we had no idea if he had a wife or family but at least it was only one witness.

The hardest part was explaining the presence of a six legged cat, who had, remarkably, managed to stay quiet throughout so as not to alert Bill to his hidden nature. Isabella explained the cat was a rescue cat that had been born deformed due to its mother being exposed to some kind of toxic waste. She was vague on the details, insisting she didn't know any more than that, it was a ridiculous story but Bill seemed to swallow it, he even laughed at one point saying we would have to explain the shed trick to him.

Alex winked at him and said "Magicians never reveal their secrets."

Bill laughed again and offered everyone a drink which we happily accepted, he agreed to allow us to stay in the pub while he went down to the cellar to do whatever it is pub landlords do in their cellars.

When he had left the room we sat down as far from the bar as possible.

"That was close" I breathed a sigh of relief.

"Indeed, we are lucky Izzy is able to reassure people with her verbal skills" Calvin said, sipping from his whiskey.

"You did all right yourself darling" Isabella responded, chinking her glass against his.

"Well done everyone" Tarquin said quietly "Our mission is still on. Our research suggests the best time for you two to get captured is during the night when the warehouses are mostly abandoned".

"And you're sure this is going to work?" I asked nervously.

"I have no idea" he said "But it's all we've got!"

I sighed and nodded taking a large gulp of my beer. We all sat in silence for a few minutes when Calvin spoke up.

"Perhaps we should retire to my camper to continue our plan, the landlord is sure to return shortly" He said. We all agreed and made our way out the back door, Alex shouted down to thank the landlord who called back something I couldn't hear.

We all bundled into Calvin's van which luckily had not been towed from the pub car park, the four of us humans sat along the two bench seats and Tarquin sat on the centre table.

"Let us test our communicators" He said motioning a paw to Isabella who produced a small bag from her coat and laid the contents out on the table.

"These devices will allow us to communicate with each other from a considerable distance apart" he slid the two small black squares to me and Alex "these go behind your ears, they will self-stick and be totally undetectable once fitted" he continued.

Alex took one of the devices, it looked like a tiny SIM card from a mobile phone and reached up to put it behind his ear, the instant it touched skin it adhered itself and turned into the matching skin tone.

"Woah!" I said

"What?" Said Alex.

"It's invisible! It's totally blended in with your skin!" I said.

"Show me!" Alex said excitedly.

I picked up the second device and repeated what he had done, making sure he could see while I did it.

"That is awesome!" He said.

"Glad you like them" Tarquin said and he slid another two of the cards towards Calvin and Isabella who did as we had and attached them to behind their ears.

"Isabella, would you mind?" Tarquin said motioning to the fifth and final device. She picked it up and put it against his left ear, it morphed seamlessly into ginger fur, covering it entirely.

"With these in place we can talk to each other as if we were in the same room, I will activate them now" Tarquin waved his paw over a small innocent looking black box on the table in front of him. ""Let us test them out" he said. As he did the words he spoke echoed in my head.

"It works!" Alex shouted, we all cringed as the echo of his shout reverberated around our skulls "oops, sorry" he continued, this time whispering.

Tarquin waved his paw over the black box again "I've turned them off for now; we can activate them again once we start the mission. This contains the virus that you will need for the mission." Tarquin slid a small box over to me, I put it in my top pocket and nodded.

"Now, Jack, Alex, do you have everything you need?"

Alex and I looked at each other and shrugged. "Not sure what else we need except a bad ass gun." He grinned.

"You know that's not possible, you are much more likely to be killed on the spot of they suspect any sign of a weapon" Tarquin explained, Alex sighed resignedly.

"Will he be able to take his good luck charm?" I asked Tarquin who looked up me quizzically and then got what I was hinting at.

"I see no reason why not; they will not kill someone just for carrying a doll" He replied.

"Oh cool" said Alex "It's been in my pocket this whole time anyway." He proceeded to pull the ugly doll from out of one of the many pockets the jumper suits provided. I shivered at the sight of it, it really freaked me out but I knew if it could do what Tarquin had said it could do we might need it later that night.

"Very well, it seems we are all prepared." Tarquin spoke "Calvin, would you be so kind as to drive us to the location we agreed upon?"

"Certainly" replied Calvin and made his way to the front of the van, Isabella scooped Tarquin under her arm and joined Calvin in the cabin.

Alex and I sat back.

"You ready for this mate?" He asked.

"I guess. You realize we might die tonight?" I said, trying to make him see the gravity of the situation.

"Meh, we'll be fine" He said, his carefree attitude completely unfazed. The van started off and we drove off into the night.

34

Calvin parked the van up behind a large building and pulled up a map of the area on his phone.

"We are here" he said, pointing at the map "and this is the warehouse district you need to be seen in" he indicated a location about half a mile from where we were currently parked.

"You will have to walk the rest of the way, we don't want the enemy to get suspicious" Tarquin added.

"No problem!" Said Alex and leapt up from his seat.

"Are you boys sure about this?" Isabella asked.

"Not really" I started to say but Alex interrupted me

"We're good!" He said, slapping me on the back. I sighed and the two of us got out of the van. Good lucks were issued all round before the door shut behind us and it was just the two of us.

"Let's go stop an invasion!" Alex said cheerily marching forwards, I followed with less enthusiasm.

As we walked along the deserted London streets I suddenly heard a voice in my head.

"Can you hear me Jack?" It was Tarquin coming in over the communicator behind my ear. I jumped slightly before realizing what was happening.

"Um....yeah" I mumbled, unsure how this worked. Alex looked at me weird and I motioned to the device behind my ear, he understood and nodded.

Tarquin then tested the device on Alex who responded with "Affirmative captain!"

"Good, all appears to be in order" Tarquin replied to both of us, ignoring

Alex's joviality. "We will be able to hear everything you say but we will only talk when we need to relay information."

"Understood." I said, feeling weird to have a voice inside my head. We walked on in light conversation to distract us from the upcoming ordeal.

"Have you pooed today?" Alex asked.

"What?" I looked at him curiously.

"It's just I haven't pooed today yet, you know I can't poo in strange places and we have been in some pretty strange places lately!" He laughed

I laughed with him "Yes I had a poo when we were off planet, the toilets there are amazing."

"Yeah I saw them when I tried to go, all high tech with music and mood lighting, but I still couldn't go. Now I'm worried I'll need a poo during this adventure and have nowhere to go." Alex looked concerned.

"I wouldn't worry about it, I'm sure we will both shit ourselves when if we get captured!" We both laughed at this and carried on walking.

"So…" I started "Lexa hey?"

"Ah man she is great, we spent all night chatting. I can't wait to see her again" The smile on his face said he meant it.

"Just chatting?" I elbowed him gently in the ribs.

"Yep. It was the best night of my life" He did a little comical skip.

"I'm pleased for you mate, just worried about the fact she is from another planet"

"I'm not worried, love conquers all" He said.

"Fair enough, I wish you both the best" I raised my hand and we high-fived.

We arrived at what had to be the warehouse district, large dark buildings loomed over us. The only light came from a few security lamps dotted around the area, it was clear this place was dead at night; we had been assured no workers would arrive until early the following morning.

We stood for a while until Alex said "What do we do now?"

The voice in our head told us to look like we were doing something.

"Like what?" I asked.

"Just look busy" this time it was Isabella's voice in our head.

Alex looked around for a bit then waved me over to him, he began pointing at roofs of buildings, he pulled out his phone and showed me pictures he had taken of random things, mostly cats and dogs as well as multiple photos of his own screen as he was constantly taking accidental screen shots. He pointed at the phone and then back at the building in front of us. It was the perfect impression of someone who knew what they were doing. Only I seemed to think we had no clue but I nodded and followed Alex's lead.

We were so engrossed in our charade that neither of us heard someone approaching us from behind. Suddenly I felt the sharp jab of a needle in my neck and everything went black.

35

It was the summer holidays before our final year at university was due to start, Anne and I decided we would pool our money and take a trip to a Spanish island, nothing special just a week's break in a sunny resort. I didn't know at the time it would end up being a nightmare vacation.

The first few days were amazing; we spent the mornings in bed, the afternoons either by the pool or on the beach. The evenings were spent drinking sangria in the local bars and just adoring our time together.

On the fourth day we decided to take a mini cruise operated by the hotel tourist department, we got up early and boarded the boat along with three other couples. The plan was to cruise around the shores for a while before a lunch was provided on a nearby beach but we never made it that far.

It was about an hour into the cruise and we were having a wonderful time, Anne was full of life and loving the breeze blowing through her, now blue, hair. She suggested we get some drinks so I agreed to go to the mini bar provided and got us a couple of cans of local lager. When I returned to the back of the boat Anne was nowhere to be seen, thinking she must have wandered around the boat I strolled around looking for her, asking the other couples if they had seen her. No one had.

Having walked the whole of the boat I was starting to get worried, I went to the driver of the boat and told him what had happened. He stopped the boat and came to look, by this point all the other people on board were helping scour the boat for Anne.

It didn't take long before it became obvious she was no longer on the boat with us, I screamed and shouted and insisted we turn around and look for her in the water. The boat went back to where we were when I last saw her but there were just miles and miles of ocean and no Anne to be seen. The coast guard was called and did their best scouring the area but no sign of her could be found, eventually it got too dark and despite my protesting they called off the search and took me back to the mainland.

Back in my hotel room I couldn't stand the empty feeling and I stayed up all night walking through the lonely streets, somehow convincing myself she would be out there somewhere. But of course I'm not so lucky; I returned to my room a broken man and promptly collapsed on the bed in tears. I must have finally fallen asleep at some point because I was awoken by a banging on the door, the police had arrived to take my statement. I insisted we go back out on a boat and search for Anne but they assured me everything possible was being done.

The police quizzed me for several hours, the detective in charge spoke good English and was ultimately convinced that nothing sinister had occurred and the incident was recorded as an accident. He left me for a while, the tears never seeming to dry up, when he returned he informed me that the coast guard had not discovered anything on their search but they would be out looking until it was dark.

That evening I sat in the hotel bar drowning my sorrows, foregoing the lively fun of sangria and instead sticking to neat bourbon. The detective found me and sat down next to me. He explained that there had been no sign of Anne either in the sea or any of the beaches nearby, with his head held low he informed me that there was no point in further searching and I would have to accept that she was gone.

I voiced my protestations but in my heart I knew it was true. I had found my one true love and the cruel world had taken her away from me. I spent the rest of the week renting out boats and going out to where I had last seen Anne, of course it was pointless; even if I could pinpoint exactly where we had been the tides would have moved her on by now.

Eventually my money ran out and I had to admit defeat, I took my flight home as planned, the empty seat next to me only widened the empty feeling inside. I had contacted Alex whilst away and he met me at the airport; I collapsed into his arms sobbing uncontrollably, the drive home was a silent one. I was not feeling like talking and Alex, for the first time since I met him, not knowing what to say.

He dropped me off at my parents' house promising to come see me the next day, I cried some more with my parents before going to my room and curling up in devastation.

36

I woke up with a banging headache and the world was blurred and dark, for a minute I thought I had dreamed everything and was waking up with another hangover, then I realized I had something over my head. I could hear voices and footsteps around me.

"This one's awake" one voice said.

"Uncover him and we can interrogate him" the other said, light flooded my eyes as the bag or was removed from my head, I was in a small office which I assumed was part of one of the warehouses, my hands were handcuffed behind my back. I blinked rapidly and shook my head looking up to face my captors.

Despite all I had seen in recent days I was not prepared for what stood before me, there were two men, at least I think they were male, with mostly human bodies, two arms, two legs but it was their heads that made me gasp

They had the heads of dolphins, that's the only way I can describe it. Smooth bluish grey skin, tiny black eyes and wide mouths filled with what looked like hundreds of small teeth. The skin on their arms also seemed to be the same grey texture, it appeared to glisten slightly as if they had just come out of the water, but that may have been my imagination going overtime and seeing what you expect when you see a dolphin.

"You're....dolphins?" I stuttered.

"What the hell is a dolphin?" One of them said to the other.

"No idea. It doesn't matter; we are asking the questions here!" The other one said as he turned to me and held a large fist up to my face.

"Who are you and what are you doing here?" He grabbed the neck of my jumper suit roughly; I realized Alex was sat nearby, still wearing the same outfit as I with a sack over his head. He appeared to still be out cold.

"We just work here" I blurted out "What's going on?" I tried to sound frightened which didn't require much acting.

"Why are you here at this time? The place is closed!" The dolphin man yelled at me.

"We were just doing some overtime, need to get this job done for the boss asap" I said, trying to sound convincing though I felt anything but.

The two dolphin men walked away and began whispering to each, the appeared to be wearing some kind of uniform, black trousers and a black body warmer with red stripes on the chest and some symbols underneath each stripe, alien text maybe? Whatever it was I couldn't read it. They nodded to each other and exited the room through the only door. I waited a few moments for them to come back but heard nothing so I whispered.

"Alex? Psst are you awake?" No response. Clearly handcuffs were the one thing my ability was useful for and I easily popped one hand off and bought my other hand around to my front where I reattached my hand and used it to pull the other one off and lose the cuffs. I sneaked over to Alex and took the bag off his head.

"Alex, wake up" I shook him vigorously and eventually felt him begin to stir, he looked up at me bleary eyed.

"Did we win?" He drawled.

"Not yet, but the plan worked I think, we have been captured. And get this, the X-Borgs are half dolphin!" I said, with that his eyes popped open.

"No way!" He said "Which half?"

"Well just the head as far as I can tell, be hilarious if it was the bottom half though, you know, if they weren't planning on killing us all." I spoke quietly.

"That's awesome, a race of dolphin people" He chuckled softly.

"They might not all be dolphin people, I've only seen two so far. Either way we need to find their mainframe and get this virus in place." As I spoke a distant voice rolled around my head, I couldn't quite make out what it was saying until suddenly it came in loud and clear.

"Jack!" It was Tarquin "Can you hear me now?"

36

"I hear you Tarquin" I replied, trying to keep my voice down.

"Thank the maker for that, we thought we had lost you and had to change frequencies. Have you managed to release the virus?"

"Not yet, we got knocked out and only just woke up" I said.

"Ask him if he knew they were dolphin people?" Alex said.

"I can hear you too Alex, what's a dolphin?" Tarquin seemed genuinely confused.

"Why has no one heard of dolphins?" I muttered.

"That's not important right now; do you know where you are?" It was Isabella talking this time.

"My guess is we are in an office belonging to one of the warehouses, we were handcuffed, I've got out of mine OK but Alex is still cuffed." I said.

"I see. Alex, use the suit to free yourself, remember it shrinks to fit the wearer? Well it also expands when you want it to. Concentrate on making it as the sleeves as big as possible" Tarquin explained.

"How will that work?" I asked "These are steel handcuffs, fabric suits aren't going to break them"

"Trust me, those suits are stronger then you think" Tarquin sounded confident so I nodded at Alex who squeezed his eyes shut and concentrated hard. After a few moments the arms began to expand and soon filled the armholes of the cuffs, then they continued. Somehow the material of the suit was straining against the metal with tremendous force and I could actually see the cuffs starting to stretch. Eventually they became wide enough that the internal lock couldn't cope any more and they simply popped open. Alex relaxed and the suit began to shrink down to become the perfect fit once more.

"Awesome! I love this suit!" He said loudly.

"Shh, we don't want to alert the X-Borgs!" I whispered.

"Right, OK, sorry." Alex whispered back "But I'm never taking this suit off" he smiled.

"Are you free Alex?" Tarquin asked.

"Yep, free and ready to rumble!" Alex replied.

"Good. Now can you see where the mainframe is located?" as Tarquin asked this I made my way to the door and peered out the small window sunk into it.

"It looks like we are in an upstairs room, the main warehouse is below us but I can't see anything else from here." I said.

"You're going to have to risk going out of the room I'm afraid" Tarquin sadly.

I sighed "Okay" slowly I pushed the door open enough to peer out, seeing no movement I chanced opening it further. There was a small balcony area in front of the office and a metal stairway leading up to is, we were fairly high up and could see below us. The main warehouse was pretty much empty except for a large storage crate in the middle of the room, standing outside this was one of the dolphin men who I had seen before, he appeared to be armed with some kind of gun and was clearly acting as a guard to whatever was going on inside the crate. I stepped back inside, softly closing the door and explained to Alex and Tarquin what I had seen.

"We need a distraction" said Alex.

"I have an idea" I said and went over to the pc on the office desk, sure enough the pc had controls for the main doors of the warehouse. I told Alex to peer out the door and watch to see what happens. Clicking on the open button on the screen a loud metal screeching noise could be heard from down below.

"The big door is opening" Alex said "The dolphin dude is going to see what's going on. Man, how weird are they!"

"Is anyone else coming out of the crate?" I asked.

"Yeah another dolphin bloke has joined the first one, they are looking at the door, do we chance going for it?"

"I'll make the door go down and back up again, that should distract them long enough, but we don't know how many more are inside the crate." I said, clicking the buttons on the console.

"We have to risk it" Alex said and eased himself out the door before I could protest.

I sneaked out after him, he was already halfway down the stairs, I tried my best to catch up without making too much noise. Luckily the sound of the main door was making enough noise to cover anything else up. At the bottom of the stairs we were fairly hidden from the guards inspecting the entrance which allowed us to sneak around behind the container. Alex made various hand gestures like we were in the army, I just gave him a confused look to convey I had no idea what he was on about, he shrugged his shoulders and approaching the entrance of the container he peered around to look inside. He gave me the thumbs up and rounded the corner and into the container, checking no one else was around I followed him.

Inside the container was an array of machinery, various flashing lights and beeping sounds emitted from what had to be the mainframe of their operation.

"This must be it" Alex whispered to me, then to Tarquin he said "How do we input the virus?"

"You just need to adhere it to the side of the mainframe, it will stick and camouflage itself in the same way the communicators did. I can do the rest from here" Tarquin explained. I took the small box he had given me from my pocket and opening it up, the device itself was no bigger than a stamp and looked like a tiny circuit board. I pressed it against the side of the large machinery, putting it somewhere it would not be obviously seen. I needn't have worried; as soon as it was attached it took on the effect of the material it was stuck too and became invisible to the naked eye.

"It's done" I whispered.

"Good, I'll begin uploading the virus" Tarquin replied.

"Now get the hell out of there you two" Isabella said in our heads.

"Roger that" Said Alex, we turned around to leave and were immediately face to face with the two dolphin men.

"Ah crap" I managed to say before the back of gun was filling my vision.

37

Once again I awoke with a banging headache; I was getting sick of this. Looking around I appeared to be in a small metal room, empty with an opening at one end, I stood up and walked to the opening, as I did red beams shot out from the side of the walls barring my exit.

"Damn" I muttered.

"Proper Star Trek shit isn't it?" I heard Alex's voice from what had to be the cell next door.

"Where are we?" I asked him

"Your guess is as good as mine, I woke up in here a few minutes ago, been trying to figure out the laser beams. Be warned, they give you a nasty shock if you touch them" He replied.

"You touched them?" I asked.

"Of course, had to figure out what they were for, would not recommend" He laughed, his spirit not even dampened by our predicament.

"Glad you are not worried!" I said back.

"Oh I am worried about one thing" He said "There's no toilet in my room and I still haven't pooped." It was my turn to laugh.

"I think that's the least of our worries" I said, then another voice joined in with our conversation.

"They will let you out soon to eat and use the facilities" the voice said, it sounded vaguely familiar but I couldn't quite place it.

"Who's that?" Asked Alex.

"Just another prisoner, there are a few of us in here" the voice spoke.

"I'm Alex, and my friend in the next cell is Jack" Alex said.

"I'd say it's nice to meet you but under the circumstances..." she trailed off "My names May".

"Howdy May, how long have you been here?" Alex asked.

"Not long, it's hard to tell in here, what day is it?" May asked.

"Monday" I said, and then added "the 11th".

"That's weird, I could swear I had only been here a few days but last I remember it was the 22nd of June.

"Um...I hate to break it to you but its November" Alex said.

"What?! That can't be right! I know I haven't been here five months! Are you sure?" She asked.

"Yep. 11th November 2022" Alex stated, there was silence from the cell.

"You all right?" I asked.

"No, not really. The last day I remember was June 22nd 2007" May sounded totally broken. "This can't be right"

"How did you get here?" I asked.

"I was walking home from work one day, next thing I know I woke up here; I swear it was only three of four days ago." May replied, I still felt I had heard her voice before and it was making my crazy trying to think of it.

"May, this will sound odd but I feel like I know you." I said.

"Really? I used to be a teacher, where are you from?" She asked. Suddenly it hit me, memories came flooding back and I knew where I had heard that voice before, it hadn't hit me at first because I never knew her first name.

"Miss Barden?" I said shakily.

"How did you know that?" She asked shocked.

"It's me, Jack Harris, you used to tutor me when I was younger" I explained, again there was silence for a few moments.

"Jack? That's can't be. Jack is a fourteen year old boy, I saw him the day I arrived here. What are you playing at?" She was angry.

"I swear it's me, I'm twenty seven now. I can't explain what is going on but it really is me. Remember how I used to hate maths and would draw little alien men all over my homework? You used to give the pictures marks out of ten in red pen."

"This....this is not possible. I'm so confused." May was in shock.

"You're not the only one" I said.

"Can anyone hear me?" I heard Alex say and was about to respond when I realized he was trying to contact someone through his communicator. I touched my hand to the space behind me ear and could still feel the device in place.

"Tarquin? Calvin? Isabella?" I said out loud. There was no response, not even a crackle.

"Have you two gone mad?" May asked.

"We have…er…radio things, we're trying to contact our friends" I said "But I'm getting nothing, Alex?"

"Same here, nothing at all" he said.

"We're probably too far away" May said "Assuming your friends are still on Earth.

"They are….wait…what?!" Alex said.

"Sorry I forgot you wouldn't know yet, we are not on Earth any more."

38

"Holy crap we're in space....we are in space this time right?" Alex asked

"It would appear we are" I said staring out the large window of what I can only assume was an alien spaceship. We had been released from our cells and marched at gunpoint into a circular room with tables and chairs, the dolphin men locked us in and left.

"Miss Barden" I started.

"I think you can call me May now Jack, I can't believe it's really you, I saw you as a boy only a few days ago"

"It's me alright Miss Barden....May" I corrected myself "Do you have any idea how we ended up in space?"

"None at all, like you I just woke up in one of those cells, every day they take us to this room and feed us, then at night we are shuffled off to our cells again" May said.

"Us? There's more people here?" I asked

"Oh yes there are a few humans on board, all captives of these weird dolphin things, they should be joining us soon" She turned to look at Alex "By the way, the bathrooms are through that door" She pointed to indicate where she meant.

"Thanks!" Alex shouted as he ran through the door.

"How are you so calm?" I asked May when he had gone.

"I'm not. Inside I am trembling, it's just this is so unreal I don't think my brain can comprehend that it's really happening. I thought I was dreaming for the longest time at first" she said. I nodded and we stood staring out the window, the view was impressive despite the circumstances. I could see stars and even planets in the distance, I wondered if one of them was earth and if I would ever set foot on it again.

Alex returned from the bathroom "Aah, that's better" he said.

"Did you poop?" May laughed.

"Oh no, not in a public loo, I just really needed to wee" He replied. "It's actually quite nice in there, you know, for an alien race that enslaves humans I mean".

"Well I need to go now, excuse me" I went through the door into the bathroom, the lights came on as I entered and I was greeted by red walls, floor and ceiling. There was a row of sinks but I could see no taps, the toilet itself was a grand golden throne. I only needed a wee but I couldn't resist sitting down to try the throne out, besides it was easier to lower the jumpsuit completely, the gold felt warm to the skin and I sat there for a few minutes to try and sort my thoughts out.

We needed a plan, some way off this ship but how could we defeat the X-Borgs? They had guns and we just had my ability to detach limbs...not very helpful in this situation. Plus even if we did somehow overcome them we are floating in space and had no idea how to get home. It all seemed pretty hopeless and my mind was insisting I just let events fold out in front of me.

I stood up and walked over to the sink, staring at it wondering how it worked I opted to just wave my hands around the sink area, sure enough a spout appeared from out of the side and warm water poured out. I washed my hands and a second spout came out which provided warm air which was powerful enough to instantly dry my hands.

Walking back into the room I could hear more voices, the other captives must have arrived, I wondered what my jail mates would be like, no matter what I thought I wasn't in anyway prepared for what waited for me in that room.

Standing around Alex were two new people to the room, upon seeing who they were my mouth dropped open in shock. The two people turned to look at me and there, standing in front of me was Steve, my old bodyguard friend and Mrs. Williams, the mother of my childhood friend who had been the first to experience my hand trick.

"What the hell?" I said

""Whoa, you look just like a kid I used to work with!" Said Steve, coming over to meet me.

"It is him" May said "Just older"

"What? That can't be right, he's only 17, I saw him the other week" Steve was studying me.

"Steve? I can't believe it. How are you all here?" I stumbled over my words.

"What's going on? Do you all know each other or something?" Mrs. Williams was asking.

"It's me Mrs. Williams, Jack Harris, I used to know your son Stephen, remember?" I said.

"Nonsense. Jack Harris is an 11 year old boy, what is going on?" She said unbelieving.

"Is this some kind of elaborate prank?" Steve asked.

"It really is me guys, I don't know how to explain it but somehow you have all been pulled out of time. Steve here was my bodyguard back when I was a teenager, May used to be my personal tutor and Mrs. Williams was... is, a mum to one of my childhood friends. I know it sounds unreal but there is a lot going on here" I tried to explain as best I could, I didn't know what was happening myself but it seemed to somehow revolve around me.

"Last time I saw Jack Harris he played a horrible prank on me at his birthday party, that was two weeks ago so you can't be him!" Mrs. Williams said.

"Was the prank a fake hand?" Steve asked.

"Well, yes, how did you know that?" Mrs. Williams stared at him.

"Jack, if it really is you can you show us what you can do to prove it?" Steve looked at me.

I nodded and with my right hand I detached my left and waved it at everyone.

"It's him" Said Steve, May nodded; Mrs. Williams fainted, only narrowing avoiding the floor by being caught by Steve as she fell.

39

I spent the year after losing Anne in a depressive state, doctors prescribed me more meds and I chose to also self-medicate with weed and booze. I quit university; it seemed pointless without Anne at my side. Family did their best to encourage me to carry on and I would put on an act to show I was fine, even managed to land a dead-end job in a factory just to keep my mind occupied.

Alex helped as best he could, he took me out drinking and tried to keep me positive, slowly I began to regain some form of normality to my life. I was still hurting inside, I was still drinking myself to sleep but I was holding down a job and managing a semblance of a social life.

I became obsessed with other projects to keep my busy, my first being to get Alex to quit smoking. I knew it was hypocritical of me to be drinking so much on the one hand and telling him he needed to quit the cigs on the other but it gave me a mission. Surprisingly he took to it extremely well, I thought at first he was just doing it to placate me but after a while it became obvious he was serious about quitting. I bought him his first vape pen with some bubble-gum flavoured liquid which he thought was the best thing ever.

My other projects included learning to drive, getting my first car, building miniature models I would buy off eBay and teaching myself the inner workings of computers. I became pretty good at it, so much so I managed to land a job in a small pc repair store where I excelled at work that didn't involve much customer action.

As time went on it got easier, I never forgot about Anne but the hurting was more internalized, I still had the odd night crying to myself, a beer in my hand but these became less and less frequent.

Driving on road trips with Alex became a big reason to at least have some time sober. He moved into a shared house with others and I found myself spending a lot of time there.

It was during this period that I gave up my non-disclosure agreement and started showing off my ability to others. I never mentioned the facility and no one from there every came knocking at my door to arrest me so I guess they either weren't monitoring me any more or had decided it was not such a big deal.

It became well known by people in my immediate circle that I could detach body parts when I wanted, the funny thing was people didn't believe it was real, even some of those who saw me do it in front of their eyes thought it was just some clever magic trick.

A reporter tried to do a story on me and I downplayed it a little, saying it was just one hand I could detach, but even then his editor thought it was bullshit and wouldn't print it for fear of being ridiculed.

Life was by no means a bed of roses, two years had now passed since Anne and she was still always on my mind, but it became bearable, by throwing myself into work and hobbies I distracted myself enough to function in society.

At 22 I was making reasonable money as an IT consultant, the government money had been paid directly to me since I turned 21 so I was making enough to move out of my parents and into a little flat above a shop, it was a Laundromat when I first moved in, it soon closed down and reopened as the Asian supermarket that is still there to this day. Alex would insist on me bringing him a different Asian snack each week, I would pick the weirdest looking thing I could find but he always ate it. I was too set in my simple ways to try most of them and those that I did were pretty disgusting to me bland pallet.

My work was all remote and all done via email which meant I rarely had to interact with anyone in person which suited me just fine as I preferred to avoid other people as much as I could, I longed for the times I used to sit in the facility woods by myself and pretend I was the last person on earth.

40

Mrs. Williams had been laid down on the floor to recover, no dolphin men had appeared to see what was going on so I came to the conclusion they either weren't watching or they just didn't care. A machine on the wall spat out metal trays with some kind of slop on them, May informed us this was breakfast, Alex tucked right in and eventually hunger got the better of me and I tried a little of the unrecognizable food. It was surprisingly delicious and I wolfed down the rest of my portion, the others did the same.

From what I could ascertain Mrs. Williams had been here the longest out of our misfit group, approximately two weeks, after that arrived Steve who estimated he had been here about a week. May was the last to arrive and she thought she had only been here a few days, none of them could explain how they all appeared to have come from different years. The one thing they all had in common however was me. They had all known me as I was growing up and had all disappeared from my life at some point or another, I thought they had just moved on with their own lives but if what they were saying is true they had been snatched out of time and bought into the future.

"So how do we know what year it really is?" Said Alex "After all everyone here thinks it's a different year so we might be wrong as well." He made a good point, the truth was there was no way of knowing if he and I had been sent into the future as well, all we could agree on was that each of us came from a different point in time.

"I'm ever so sorry about that" We turned to see Mrs. Williams sitting up "After being abducted by dolphin like aliens you'd think nothing would shock me" she laughed and Alex helped her to her feet. "I think it all just hit me at once". She came and sat with us and I offered to get her a tray of food, she declined, saying she didn't feel like eating right now. We caught her up on the conversation we had had, talking carefully to not shock her any further, she dutifully nodded throughout and seemed to be taking it all in.

"So. We're fucked is what you're saying?" She said eventually.

"Mrs. Williams! Language!" I laughed.

"Oh please, we are a practically all the same age now, and call me Beth" she replied.

"Glad to see you are feeling better Beth, I'm Alex, of course you know Jack" Alex declared.

"Yes, well at least I did, he looks nothing like that eleven year old boy I saw two weeks ago, well what seems like two weeks ago to me. How scary is it that it's been over fifteen years" She shook her head in disbelief.

"Jack, as you seem to be the common link between us, do you have any idea what they want with us?" Steve asked me.

"Not exactly, I'll tell you what I know so far but it's going to be hard to believe" I replied.

"I think we all need to know" said Steve. I nodded and explained to them the whole story of how we had ended up here. Starting with the first time we saw Tarquin then meeting Calvin and Isabella and our eventual trip to the other world. Lastly I detailed our plan to sabotage the X-Borgs, at this point Alex chimed in to say that he had named them that, and about our trip to the warehouse.

"And then we woke up here, I have no idea how they got us from that warehouse to this ship, I assume they have some sort of portal like Tarquin's people" I finished.

There was quiet in the room before Mrs. Williams, sorry Beth, spoke up.

"Well that's just fucked up" she sat back in her chair. I couldn't help but agree.

"The question is" said Alex "What happened next? Did the X-Borgs destroy humanity? Did we stop them in time? We don't even know how long has passed since we left earth."

"We need answers and the only way I can see of getting them is contacting Tarquin, if he's even still alive" I said.

"Our communicators aren't working, does that mean no one is left to answer or are we too far away or what?" Alex asked.

"No idea. These aliens must have some sort of communication devices that reach earth so they can talk to each other. We just have to find it". I said

"How do you plan on doing that? We are only let into this room outside our cells and there appears to be no way out with an armed guard". May waved her arms around the room. She was right, there were only two doorways, the one to the toilet and the one we came in through, I stood up and tried the second of these. The door was locked, of course it was, I walked around the room inspecting every nook and cranny, the only other thing I found was a small square door set into the wall.

"Where does this go?" I asked no one in particular.

"That's where the used trays go" said Steve "Here, I'll show you" he picked up his empty tray, opened the small door and put it inside, closing the door we heard a whoosh noise, when he opened the door again the tray was gone.

"We don't know where they go, could be anywhere" He shrugged his shoulder.

"Besides it's too small for any of us to fit in so I'm not sure how it can help us". May said.

"Yeah, you're right. I'll keep thinking." I continued walking around when Alex came up to me and whispered.

"Remember what that alien doctor said about you being able to control your separated parts? Your hand would fit in that chute."

"Yeah but you know I don't know how to do that" I sighed dejectedly.

"Have you ever really tried?" He asked.

"Well...no I suppose not, the facility ran all sorts of tests and trials but we deduced they were essentially dead limbs when not attached" I said.

"Ah but if they were dead wouldn't they start to rot and smell rancid after being away from you for so long? You know, on the occasions you lose your hand" Alex made sense; my hands had always been in perfect condition whenever I had retrieved it, even after a week of being lost.

"OK, so maybe they don't 'die' exactly but I still can't control them" I said.

"Just try it, what have we got to lose?" Alex clapped me on the back, I shrugged my shoulders and sat down at the table, I was about to take my hand off when I looked at Beth.

"You're not going to faint again are you?" I asked.

"No I think I've seen it all now, go ahead" she laughed and watched intently as I pulled my left hand off and laid it on the table.

"Now" said Alex "Think about moving your hand, try and move a finger" I did as he said, staring at the hand, willing it to move. Nothing happened.

"It's not working!" I said slumping down in my seat.

"Maybe you are thinking to hard" Alex said "Just try to relax and pretend the hand is still attached to your arm. Don't try to mentally move it, just act as if you could still feel it" I looked at him with a raised eyebrow but agreed to give it another go.

I sat up, closed my eyes and moved my stump to the table, I began to imagine the hand was still attached and I was drumming my fingers. After a few moments I was ready to give up when I heard a tapping.

"Holy crap!" Said Alex "It's working!"

Slowly I opened my eyes but continued concentrating on tapping my disembodied fingers, sure enough the hand was moving, gently tapping out a rhythm on the table. My eyes shot opened and I sat forward, as I did so hand stopped moving and became lifeless again.

"What happened?" Said Steve

"I don't know it just stopped working" I said.

"It's because you stopped relaxing when you saw it work" May said "It looks like your talent only works when you are not thinking about it, try again" I did as she asked, once again closing my eyes and thinking only about using the hand as any normal person would. Sure enough the hand started its tapping again, this time I imagined moving the hand forward in a walking manner.

"He's doing it!" Said Steve "the hand is moving!"

I decided to chance opening my eyes but I did so slowly and relaxed, keeping my mind on moving the hand. There it was, my own left hand walking across the table like a small animal, I let out a little laugh but kept my concentration.

"I suggest you practice for a while, meanwhile we can try and see if there is any way this can help us" May said, I nodded and started to practice, while I was concentrating on this from the corner of my eye I noticed the ugly doll was climbing out of Alex's pocket, I looked around but the others were all deep in conversation and no one noticed as the doll scuttled across the room and grabbed climbed under one of the food trays. Unaware it was even there Steve picked up the tray and went to chuck it down the chute, as he did I saw the doll was hanging on to the underside, it turned to me and winked as it disappeared down the chute with the used tray.

I had no idea what the little bugger was up to and I didn't have time to worry about it so I spent the next two hours moving my hand in various ways Alex helped by standing next to me suggesting movements.

"Have it pick your nose!" Was one "Give me the middle finger!" Was another, I obliged until the suggestions got a bit too personal.

"I think I've mastered it now" I said triumphantly reattaching the hand to my arm.

"Now send it down the rubbish chute and find us a way out of here" Alex suggested.

"I don't think that would help us" I said.

"Why not?"

"Well it's no good sending my hand down if I can't see where it's going!"

"Oh. Yeah. Good point" He looked saddened that all that training wasn't going to help.

"We think we have a way you can help but it will have to wait till we are back in our cells." Steve said.

41

The rest of the day had been spent sat in that same round room, chatting and staring into space. At various points food was made available and a machine provided water to drink whenever we wanted it. Eventually the guards arrived and escorted us back to our cells, Alex, myself and May to one block and the others to a different block of cells. When the guard had left us alone it was time to try Steve's idea.

"You two ready?" I asked Alex and May, they both responded in the positive. I detached my left hand and 'walked' it towards the cell entrance, sure enough the red lasers appeared as it approached but there was just enough room to slip the hand under the lowest beam. My hand was free, now came the hard part, from what May had said she could see the console which the guards used when they locked us in, presumably it controlled the laser beams. It would be down to Alex to guide me to where she could see me and from there she could tell me how to get to the console.

The process took a lot longer than we anticipated with cries of "left a bit, right a bit" and so on, my hand must have looked amusing scuttling around the floor. Eventually May announced I was at the foot of the console.

"Now you have to get up to it, it's about two foot high, think you can do it?" She asked.

"I'll give it a go; we managed it in practice, just a lot harder when you can't see what you're aiming for." With that I curled the fingers of my hand underneath themselves and with all the force I could muster I flicked down. In practice I had manage to perfect this jumping motion, allowing my hand to fling itself in the air, that part was relatively easy, getting it to fling in the right direction was not so simple.

"Nearly!" Said May "Try again, this time try and move a little to the right". I did as she suggested, in total we must have tried a dozen times before finally May shrieked "Yes!"

Calming down she said "Okay, there are three buttons, if you stick out your index finger I will guide you to the one I think turns of the beams."

"You *think*? Said Alex

"Well it's hard to know for sure, I know one turns them off and one opens the outer door so the other one must turn them on. We won't know until we try" She replied. With that I did as she asked and she guided my finger to the button in question, I pushed down feeling the button on my finger, it felt like I was simply operating my hand with my eyes closed.

"Did it work?" I asked.

"Let's find out" Said Alex and next thing I knew he was stood in front of my cell grinning.

"I guess it did!" I said, May stepped out of her cell to join us.

"Well done Jack, I actually wasn't sure that would work" she patted my shoulder as we looked around the room.

"Okay we have made it this far, are we ready to enact phase two of the plan?" I asked.

"We have to try, but remember this will be the dangerous part" May said.

"I'm ready!" Said Alex and he stepped back into his cell, May and I crammed ourselves into a corner, I left my hand poised over the buttons.

"We good?" Asked Alex, we nodded in reply at which point Alex started to yell.

"Help! They've disappeared! What's happening!" He continued in this vein for some time before we finally heard the main door slide open and one of the dolphin men came in looking as furious as a dolphin face can look.

"What is going on here?" It said and then it noticed the empty cells and pulled out his gun "Where are they?" He yelled at Alex who just shrugged his shoulders, once the guard looked into May's empty cell we took our queue and the two of us rushed forward pushing him into the cell and knocking him to his feet. Before he could stand again I used my hand to press the lock button, the guard stood and rushed forward getting a nasty shock which caused the gun to fly from his hand and out into the main room. Alex, who had leapt out of his cell before I pressed the button grabbed the gun and laughed.

"Now who's in charge!" He said pointing the gun at the guard, the guard could not reply as he was currently lying unconscious on the floor of the cell having charged the laser beams with tremendous force.

"Do you even know how to use that?" I asked.

"Huh. I'm sure I'll figure it out" he replied examining the weapon.

"We need to get out of here before anyone else comes, that trick won't work twice." May said.

"Good point, do you have any idea how many more guards there are?" I asked.

"No idea, they all look the same to me" May shrugged.

"How dolphin-phobic!" Alex laughed "Although now that you mention it all dolphins do look alike."

I picked up my hand and reattaching it pressed the button to open the main door, it slid open smoothly and quietly and Alex peered around the opening.

"All clear" he whispered and we moved forward as a group. Outside was the long corridor we had been led down going off in both directions, we knew which way the canteen room was and the others had continued on further after us so we turned left.

The first door we came to had three empty cells so we continued on, finding another three rooms all with empty cells.

"Just how many people do they plan on capturing?" Asked Alex.

"Who knows, guess they like to be prepared" I said moving on, we opened the next door and at first thought it was another empty room, then I heard the sounds of crying and went in to investigate. Curled up in the corner of one of the cells was someone I couldn't make out, I went over to the console to turn off the beams.

"Hold on, we'll get you out" I pressed the button and turned around, what I saw made my mouth drop open in shock.

"Jack?" Anne said standing up, tears streaming down her face. "Oh thank god it's you!" She ran forward and threw her arms around me. I was stunned and couldn't do anything for a moment, then my arms took over and wrapped them around her shivering body, when she had calmed a little I lifted her head to see her properly.

"How is this possible?" I asked, now it was my turn to cry. "I thought you were dead?"

"Dead? We were on a boat together two hours ago, why would you think I was dead?" She replied confused.

"Oh boy, this is going to take some explaining" Alex said.

"I'm sorry to break up this reunion but we don't have time for explanations, we need to find the others" May said, scanning the corridor for any sign of guards.

I wiped my eyes and hugged Anne some more "She's right; I promise I will explain everything when we get a chance." Anne nodded then looked at my fully.

"You look different...something's changed" She looked at me quizzically, now was not the time to try and explain that I was seven years older than she thought I was, she still wore the summer dress she had on last time I had seen her.

"Soon, I'll try and explain soon, we have others we need to save" I said reluctantly, her gorgeous blue hair felt soft in my hand and I wanted nothing more than to curl up with her forever but I knew forever would not be very long if we didn't get out of this place.

"OK, yes, let's get out of here" She said wiping her eyes with my sleeve as she used to do. I took her hand and the four of us made our way down the corridor, after a couple more empty cells we finally found the others and released them, brief introductions were made without going into too much detail so as not to overwhelm Anne.

"Now what?" Asked Steve

"Well we have a gun now, I say we take over this place" Alex said, raising the gun to show everyone.

"We just need to find some kind of communication device and try to contact earth, if there still is an earth" I said, realizing what I had let slip the second my mouth opened.

"What?!" Said Anne

"Ignore him" said Alex "you know he's always doom and gloom" He laughed and slapped my back, I gave him a look that said 'thank you'.

"Come on, let's move further on, there must be something other than cells on this place" May said and as a group we snuck forward, Steve taking the lead, there were two more rooms which contained empty cells finally we came to a door that looked different.

"This must be important" whispered Steve and motioned for us to gather around the door "Alex get the gun ready, if we take them by surprise we may be able to get the drop on them."

Alex nodded and held the gun up as he lent against one side of the door, he was clearly loving this, the giant grin on his face gave it away.

"May can you be ready to press the door open button?" Steve asked, May nodded back and readied herself by the button. I stood behind Alex and held Anne's hand tightly.

"On three" Steve said softly "one, two, three" May slammed her hand on the button and the door slid open, Alex leapt in gun held high.

"Freeze mother……oh" He stopped and lowered the gun. I peered round from behind him, the room appeared to be some kind of control room with various consoles with flashing lights and beeping noises. On the floor of the room there lay three dolphin people, they did not appear to be moving.

"What the hell?" Steve said. May cautiously approached one of the aliens and nudged it with her foot, Alex aimed his gun at the body but it showed no sign of life.

"I think their dead" May said, chancing putting her hand on the creature's neck to check for a pulse.

"Do dolphins have pulses?" Alex asked, kneeling beside her.

"I assume so" replied May "But this one doesn't have one, wait, what on earth is this?" She picked up Alex's ugly doll which was lying next to the corpses of the X-Borgs, holding it with the tip of her fingers in disgust.

"Oh that's my good luck charm! It must have fallen out of my pocket when we barged in." Alex took the doll and tucked it back into his pocket; it seems the doll had bought more than just luck. Had it really killed three alien beings?

It didn't seem possible but my opinions on what is and isn't possible had certainly been tested recently.

"What is going on?" Asked Anne, clinging onto me "What even are they?"

"They're X-Borgs" said Alex as if this explained everything.

I put my hands on Anne's shoulders and looked her straight in the eye "Some really weird shit is going down, I can't explain it fully but I will try to fill you in as soon as we are safe, you trust me right?" I said.

"Yes. Of course" She nodded, there were tears in her eyes but she was managing to be strong and hold them back. I turned back to the others.

"Everyone spread out and take a console, see if you can figure out how any of this works" I said.

"I'll watch the door" said Steve.

"Good idea, remember we are looking for some form of communication device." Alex, Beth and May each took a row of consoles and began examining them, Anne and I headed for the front of the room to what seemed to be the main control area.

There was a grand chair facing the console and various buttons were on the arms of the chair, it was impossible to know which button did which.

"Everything has symbols which I assume is text but it makes no sense to me" Beth said shaking her head.

"This thing looks like it might be some kind of microphone" May said, I turned around to see what she had found, as I did I accidentally hit one of the buttons on the chair arm, a slow whirring noise started from the front of the room and we all turned to look. The white wall in front of us was becoming opaque then fully transparent; we could see space laid out before us through what was now clearly a window.

"Oh. My. God" Said Anne.

"Space baby!" Said Alex and gave a little cheer. The rest of us looked at him disapprovingly. "What?" he said, I just shook my head and went over to May.

"Do you think it's a communicator?" I asked her.

"I have no idea, but it certainly looks like you talk into it so it must be for speaking to someone. But how it works is anyone's guess" She replied.

There were various buttons and switches, all of which were marked but in symbols more like hieroglyphics than letters. I chanced flicking a switch.

"Whoa whoa! We don't know what that does!" Said Beth, rushing over.

"We are stuck in space in an alien ship, I really don't think we have a choice but to try something, anything, unless you have a better suggestion?" I said, more harshly than I should.

Beth sighed "Whatever. Just don't blame me if you open a door and we all get sucked into space!" she walked away arms in the air.

I sat down at the console and began examining each switch and button, there was no way of knowing what did what so I just started from the left and began flicking each switch and pressing each button, waiting a moment between each one to see if anything happened. The first two attempts seemed to do nothing but the third switch illuminated the screen in front of me, more of the symbols appeared, I couldn't read them but I could recognize computer code when I saw it. I pressed the next button and waited and watched the screen, more symbols appeared but I couldn't tell if anything else had happened, I was about to press another button when I heard a distant voice in my head.

"Come in Jack. Come in Alex. Is anyone still there?" It was Isabella's voice; I looked at Alex who whooped.

"They're back!" He said, the others looked at him like he had gone insane, I shushed him so I could hear, the same message was repeating over and over.

"Hello?" I said "This is Jack, is anyone listening?" the message continued for a few moments then stopped abruptly in the middle.

"Jack? Is that you?" Isabella's voice came through loud and clear.

"Yes!" I yelled "I'm here Alex is with me, is everyone OK?" I said, meanwhile I could hear Alex behind me explaining to the others about the hidden communicators we both wore.

"Oh my god it's so good to hear your voice, we are all fine, Tarquin and Calvin are just waking up to join me, where are you? What happened?"

I explained the whole story of getting kidnapped and waking up on the alien ship, I detailed meeting the others and how all of them were linked to me in some way but from different times. Calvin confirmed time had not changed for Alex and I, and only a day had passed since we were on Earth. I didn't say anything about the doll taking out the X-Borgs, I just said we found them all dead and were now in some kind of control room with alien symbols.

"Jack, Tarquin here. I heard the whole thing, this is certainly an interesting development" He said.

"Interesting is not the word I would use" I said "Can you get us out of here?"

"I believe so, but I'm not sure you're going to like what you hear." Tarquin said.

"When do I ever?" I sighed "Go on, hit me with it."

42

One Christmas, three years after losing Anne, my parents insisted I go stay with them so I wasn't alone, I told Alex my plans and he invited himself to come with me as his parents were spending Christmas on a cruise. When I phoned my parents to ask if it was okay him joining us they were delighted, they loved Alex and found him to be a charming young man (their words, not mine).

The two of us rocked up to my old house on Christmas eve, the car full of presents and bags of dirty clothes that my mum had offered to wash for me, I did have my own machine in my flat's kitchen but had limited space to hang the clothes out to dry so very rarely did I do any washing, as a consequence the amount of dirty clothes would pile up.

My mum greeted us at the door and kissed us both on the cheeks, Alex presented her with a bottle of mulled wine and she was overjoyed at the simple gesture and said she would warm it up immediately.

My dad was sat in his usual armchair, an iPad in his hand as he read the latest news headlines, he told us to come in and sit down so we did, I asked him how he was doing and he held up his hand in a 'wait' gesture, after a few moments he put the tablet down and looked over at us.

"Good to see you both" he said.

"Good to see you too Mr. Harris" Alex said

"Anything interesting?" I nodded at the tablet.

"Nah not really, I just read the headlines, don't need to read the whole articles to see that the world is screwed." He took his glasses off and set them down on the side table "What have you been up to then?"

"Not a lot, the usual, working on some computer code, same old same old" I said shrugging.

"Oh that reminds me, can you look at my computer? It doesn't seem to print any more".

"Sure dad, I'll have quick look now" I stood up and made my way to the spare room that my dad had turned into his office leaving him and Alex to chat about god knows what.

Around the walls of the small room were various family photographs, one depicted my eleventh birthday, taken before the hand incident of course. Another showed the three us on a trip to the lake district years ago, looking over the photos brought back fond memories until I came to one of Anne and I.

It was taken on that fateful holiday, the two us grinning like idiots, sangria in our hands with the sun setting on the beach behind us. I remembered asking another tourist to take the photo for us but I had no idea how it had ended up here, I called my mum in from the kitchen.

"What's up dear?" She asked poking her head around the door.

"Where did you get this picture mum?" I pointed at the photo on the wall.

"Oh. That. Well...." She paused.

"You can tell me, it's okay" I reassured her.

"Well your father was going through some old stuff and he found our digital camera, we hooked it up to his pc and looked through the photos, thinking it would be from your cousins wedding or something but you must have borrowed it when you went away. I'm sorry Jackson, we didn't mean to pry but that was such a lovely picture of you both I had to have it printed out. I honestly forgot it was in here." Mum looked ashamed.

"I see. Were there other photos?" I wasn't angry, I'd forgotten all about taking the camera with us on holiday and was curious.

"Yes, but you shouldn't put yourself through it, you were so happy in them but I know it must now be a painful memory" mum couldn't look me in the eye.

"I want to see them mum, please"

"Okay" she walked over to the computer and flicked the screen on, clicking the mouse a few times she opened up a folder of photographs. "here you go, I'll leave you to look. Do you want some mulled wine?"

"In a minute please, I'll come join you guys in the living room" I sat down at the desk and steeled myself to look through the photos.

I don't know what possessed me to want to see them; I was curious as I had never looked at them before but I think there was also a morbid side to me that wallowed in misery.

As I scrolled through the photos I thought I would burst into tears but I think I must have cried so much that nothing came any more, it was both lovely and heartbreaking to see Anne again, to see us both when we were so happy but knowing how the trip would end.

I paused on one photo, a particularly nice one of Anne holding an ice cream with blue sprinkles on it that matched her hair, she was pulling a stupid but adorable face, what had caught my eye however was what sitting on the cart of the ice cream vendor.

It was a small ugly looking doll, hard to make out from image, I didn't recall seeing it on the day I took the photo, probably some tacky souvenir the ice cream guy had been selling but for some reason I couldn't look away from it, then as I was staring at it something began to happen.

The doll was moving, ever so slightly almost imperceptibly, I rubbed my eyes and looked again; it was definitely making small movements, like it was breathing. I zoomed in on the image, it blurred slightly but the doll was still clear to see, as I stared at it the doll lifted an arm and waved at me, I sat back in shock but slowly lent forward to look again, the doll was still waving and appeared to be looking right at me.

I was so engrossed in the photo I hadn't noticed Alex had come into the room and was standing right behind me.

"Mate? You OK?" He asked causing me to jump.

"Jesus dude!" I yelped "You scared the crap out of me!"

"Sorry" he laughed "Didn't mean to frighten, what ya doing?"

"I was looking at these photos from my trip with Anne and spotted something weird"

"Ah mate you shouldn't torture yourself"

"I know, I know but look at this" I pointed to the zoomed in picture on the screen.

Alex leaned in closer to the screen "What am I looking for dude?"

"It's right there!" I said and pointed at where I had seen the doll but there was nothing there "I don't understand, it was there"

"What was?" I ignored Alex and zoomed in on the photo even more; the doll was nowhere to be seen.

"It was...uh...never mind, I must be imagining things" I sighed.

"Uh, OK. Mate it must mess you up seeing these photos, come on let's go get your parents hammered and have a laugh"

"Yeah....okay" I was still staring at the screen; Alex clicked the monitor off and patted me on the shoulder.

"I'm sure your dad won't mind if you fix the printer later" he gently nudged me to the door and I reluctantly went back to the living room. A glass of mulled wine was waiting for me and mum had laid out an array of snacks, Alex suggested we play a game and mum gleefully went to the cupboard to pull out various board games. The evening went on with many drinks and snacks being consumed, after we had all gone to bed I snuck back into the office to take one more look at the photo, the doll was definitely not there, confused and over tired, I turned the computer off and went to bed.

43

Tarquin explained that the X-Borgs had some kind of blocking device which had stopped the communicators from working; I had inadvertently turned the blocker off when I was messing around with the console. He then explained that there was no way he could teach us how to fly the ship but there was one solution which he laid out for me.

"What? Go to the X-Borgs mother ship?" I said.

"It's the only way, we can't get one of our portals on the ship you are on, the ship you are currently on is too small for us to locate and send a portal to. The mother ship on the other hand we already know where it is, we just have to get you there first". He said.

"And how do we do that?" I asked.

"The ship will have an auto return function which I can tell you how to operate, it will fly itself back to its designated port."

"And then what? We will be on a giant spaceship full of aliens trying to kill us!" I said.

"That I can't help you with, our only hope is you manage to evade the enemy long enough for us to install a portal where I can meet you and bring you home" Tarquin said sadly.

"You have to try Jack, what choice do you have?" Isabella said.

"I agree; we need you back my friends" Calvin said.

"Okay, okay, let me talk it over with the others before I decide anything" I said.

"Very well, there is one more thing I need to tell you" Tarquin said ominously.

"Oh man, what else?" I said

"The virus you planted didn't work, it seems the aliens have a way of shutting down communications with the mainframe should an infection be detected."

"Oh great, so after all this we still haven't saved Earth?" I said.

"Not yet, but you still have a chance, once on their mother ship you can sabotage them at the source. I'm sorry Jack, it's the only way to save your planet." Tarquin explained.

"Well that's just peachy" I replied "I guess we don't have much of a choice do we?"

"Not if you want to ever return home". Tarquin said, I turned to face the others.

"Did you hear all that?" I asked Alex.

"Yep, we have to take down an alien race, sounds fun!" He replied.

"That doesn't sound like my idea of fun!" Said Beth, the others agreed.

"I know this whole situation is messed up and I really am sorry that you all got dragged into this somehow or other but I'm trying to do my best with what we have to work with. I'm not going to make anyone do anything they don't want to do but we don't have a lot of alternatives right now, short of staying on this ship forever we don't have much choice." I looked around the room, everyone looked defeated, Anne put her arm around me and spoke up.

"I trust you, no matter what I'm not leaving your side" She said softly, as she did Tarquin's voice spoke in my head.

"It will take you a while to reach the planet, if you set it going now you will have plenty of time to stop if you change your mind. I will understand" He said.

"OK, that sounds like a plan" I explained to the others what he had told me and they all agreed to think about it whilst I followed Tarquin's directions to engage the auto-return.

He had me sit at the main console where I had triggered the window, Alex and Anne stood either side of me, the others were sat on the other chairs deep in thought. Tarquin talked me step by step how to initiate basic functions, it wasn't easy without being unable to read the alien script but we managed to get there in the end and we could feel the ship moving.

"That's all you need to do for now, the ship will autopilot itself to the mother ship and will dock inside it. They won't know you are in charge so it will give you a moment to figure something out." Tarquin said.

"Yeah, then got shot to pieces when we step outside the ship" I said.

"This really doesn't sound like a great plan" Steve said.

"I know, I know. I wish I had an alternative but right now this is all I've got." I said looking at the whole group. "I've been told it will take us about 24 hours to reach the mother ship, I suggest everyone gets some rest, there must be some sleeping quarters here somewhere" I replied.

"Ooh dibs on the captains room!" said Alex running out of the room to explore, reluctantly Beth, Steve and May followed him. I remained in the control room with Anne.

"It's so good to see you" I said to her hugging her tight.

"You too but I am so confused, Jack just what is happening?" She looked me deep in the eyes.

"Okay, I'll tell you what I know, one second" I reached behind my ear and peeled the communicator from my neck; I stuck it on the console where I could easily find it again.

"I'd rather just the two of us for this conversation" I said, Anne sat down next to me and nodded. "This is going to be difficult to hear, remember being on that boat in Spain?"

"Of course, it was just a few hours ago" She replied confused.

"Well for you it was, for me it was seven years ago" I paused while she took this in.

"What? That's not possible" She spoke after a few moments.

"I'm sorry, let me tell you everything." I proceeded to tell her about her disappearing from the boat and my subsequent search for her, about how she had been declared dead by accident and how I had slipped into my depressive state. She listened intently but said nothing; I could clearly see the tears welling in her eyes however. I told her how the others here with us had also disappeared from my life, although in less dramatic circumstances and that they too were all from different times.

"That's crazy" was all she said.

"It really is, and believe me I have no idea how or why it is happening" I replied.

"I believe you Jack, there's no way you just made all that up!" She attempted a laugh.

"Wait till you hear the rest!" I said.

"Oh god, there's more? Go on, may as well get it all out" She sat back in the chair and crossed her arms "I'm ready".

At this point I explained how I had developed a habit of losing my hand on drunken nights out and how on this particular morning Alex and I had stumbled across Tarquin and the portal. I told her all that had happened, even about the ugly doll and how apparently I had been chosen by yet another alien race to receive special abilities.

"Well that could come in handy" she said finally.

"It would but he doesn't seem to be in any hurry to impart this gift, although he has been secretly helping us" I told her about the guards and what I could only assume had happened to them.

"And it's a doll?" Anne asked, I nodded.

"A three inch tall doll?" I nodded again.

"A three inch tall doll that took down three armed dolphin xbug things?"

"X-Borgs" I said "And yes, at least I think that's what happened.

"Did you spike my sangria with something?" This time her laugh was more real, I laughed with her and held her tight. After a while she gently pushed me away and stared into my eyes again.

"Jack?" She said seriously.

"Yes Anne?" I replied.

"If I've been out of your life for seven years, did you....have you....you know, moved on?" She blushed

"You mean has there been anyone else?" I asked.

"Yeah, that" She said, looking away.

"No. No one" I reassured her.

"Really? Why not?" She asked looking back.

"I love you Anne and always have, after I lost you I didn't want anyone else,

43

I still don't" I said, she jumped on my lap and kissed me hard.

"Damn, you must be mega horny after seven years!" She giggled.

"Well....now that you mention it". I gave her a smirk; she took my hand and stood up.

"Come on, let's find a room" She said smiling and we walked out of the control room and down the corridor.

"OK, but remember, I'm an old man now" I said.

"I'll be gentle, maybe" she laughed again as we jogged down the hall.

44

I was rudely awoken to the sounds of some kind of alarm, I looked over and Anne was sitting up next to me, I smiled at her.

"What the hell is that racket?" was her response.

"I dunno, but we better go and find out I suppose" I said, reluctantly getting up and putting on my jumper suit. Anne dressed as well and we stepped outside the room we had found only to be nearly knocked over by Alex running past.

"What's going on?" I asked him, he spun around to talk but still kept moving.

"We're bloody docking!" He said.

"Oh shit, come on" I grabbed Anne's hand and we raced after Alex to the control room, inside the others were all ready gathered.

"How can we already be here?" I said "We were supposed to have more time!"

"No idea but here we are" Beth pointed out the window at what just had to be the mother ship. It was immense, from our position it looked like we were approaching a planet, the ship we were on suddenly seemed miniscule and insignificant.

"Oh wow" said Anne.

A blue beam of light shot out from the mother ship encircling our own little ship, we began to be drawn in towards it.

"We need to be ready!" I said.

"I took the guns off the three guards that were in here, I've dumped the bodies in the cells, that gives us four guns" Steve said.

"Do you know how to use them?" I asked.

"I think I have figured them out, who wants one and I'll show you?" Steve held out the guns.

"I'll take one" said Beth, we all looked at her. "What? I can use a gun!"

"I'll stay with Beth then Jack and Anne can take the other gun, Alex and Steve can have one each as they seem to know what they are doing" May said, Alex, Anne and I laughed.

"What's so funny?" May asked.

"The thought that Alex ever knows what he's doing, but you're right, he's a nutter but probably played more Doom then anyone I ever met" Anne said.

"I have no idea what doom is but whatever" shrugged May, I took the last gun and Steve instructed us on how he thought they worked. It seemed pretty simple but I wished we had had a chance to try them out; none of us were keen on firing a gun inside a pressurized container floating in space.

As we neared the mother ship I suddenly realized something and ran to the main console, slamming the button I had accidentally hit earlier the window dimmed until it was white again.

"No point in letting them see us straight away" I said, turning to Steve I asked "Do you have any suggestions on what we should do when we get in there?"

"Well my idea would be turn around and get the hell out of here but it seems the moment for that has gone" he thought for a second "Probably best if we send out a small party, maybe just two of us, that way at least the others can be safe on this ship while we check it out. I'd be willing to be part of the initial team."

"I can't ask you to do this, I should go, I got us into this mess" I said.

"And there is no way I am missing out on this adventure!" Alex said.

"Jack, I am still your bodyguard and no offence but I have experience in these matters" Steve was referring to his days in the military.

"I guess" I said reluctantly.

"Then it's decided, Alex and I will investigate the area, if it's safe we can come back and get the rest of you." Steve said.

"And if it's not safe?" Said May "What do we do then?"

"We wing it, if we don't come back you do whatever you can to get this ship out of here again" said Steve "Jack, Alex do you still have the communicators?" I remembered the previous day and picked mine up from the where I had stuck it.

"Yep" I said sticking it back to my ear.

"I've been chatting to Calvin" said Alex "I wondered where you were" he pointed to me. "But Tarquin said the mother ship would block comms again and it seems like he was right".

"Yeah I got nothing, except an echo of Alex's voice" I said.

"Tarquin left the com open for the two of us so we can still talk to each other, it only works a certain distance though." Alex explained.

"Guys. I think we are here" said Anne "We've stopped moving" we all stood still and could clearly feel the ship had come to a standstill.

"OK people we are a go, remember we have the element of surprise, they are not expecting armed humans to be on this ship" Steve was getting into military mode. Alex nodded and held his gun up like he was auditioning for a Bond movie.

"Good luck boys" said Beth.

"Don't die" I said, clapping Alex on the back.

"Thanks mate" he replied "Now, does anyone know where the exit is?"

Steve sighed "Am I the only one who spent his time here investigating every inch of the ship?" The rest us just shrugged and looked sheepish.

"Never mind, follow me" Steve said and we obeyed as he led us through the corridors to the rear of the ship. He stopped as he came to what was clearly a large loading bay door.

"This is the way out, the rest of you can hide here while we head out" we huddled behind a corner where we could still see the door but ready to run back if necessary.

"Ready Alex?" Steve said.

"Ready Stu!" Alex said, we all looked at him "What? Oh yeah, sorry Steve"

Steve rolled his eyes and hit the button on the side of the door, slowly part of the door opened upwards whilst the bottom part lowered to create an exit ramp.

44

"Here we go" Said Steve.

45

The rest of us peered around the corner as Steve stepped out of the ship, he looked around him then motioned for Alex to follow, we could see them descend the ramp and walk out into the main ship. From where we were positioned we couldn't see much else of the mother ship but it appeared to be shut off from the rest of a ship, Alex and Steve disappeared from view and we could do nothing but wait.

"Halt!" we heard an unfamiliar voice, this was followed by gunfire, at least that's what I guessed it was, it was different and quieter than I imagined earthly guns sound but wasn't quite the laser sounds you hear on sci-fi movies either. We froze in place waiting, after a moment Alex's head popped into view making us all jump.

"There was only one dolphin dude here and Steve dealt with him, come on down!" He said cheerfully.

I looked at Anne and the others and we proceeded to slowly make our way down the ramp. We were in a large room, I surmised it was a docking bay on account of the fact we had just docked, and there appeared to be only one doorway, unless you count the giant one our ship had flown in through. Steve was stood over one of the X-Borgs, his gun slightly smoking, the dolphin like alien was clutching a gun of his own but had never had a chance to fire it.

"This dude's like frigging Jason Bourne or something!" Alex said pointing at Steve.

"Let's not get cocky, we were lucky there was only one of them to meet us and he was totally caught by surprise". Steve picked up the dead X-Borgs gun, handed it to Anne and walked over to the door.

"This appears to be the exit into the main ship, we have no idea what is waiting for us beyond this door." He said.

"We can handle it!" said Alex who pushed the door open button on the side, it slid open and facing us was another of the X-Borgs, this time it was ready and fired upon seeing us, Alex took the shot directly in the chest, he flew backwards and Steve fired back getting the X-Borg right in the middle of it's dolphin head.

"Oh shit!" said Anne rushing over to Alex.

"That should have been me" Steve said "Stupid kid, dying for nothing". He was overwrought. Anne rolled Alex over and looked at his chest.

"Wait, there's no blood, there's not even any damage to his clothes. Are they using blanks?" She said, Steve came over to see what she was talking about, as he did Alex groaned.

"Son of a bitch!" Said Steve "You kids didn't tell me you those suits were armoured, no wonder he had no fear!"

"Um...we didn't know that" I said

"It's true" moaned Alex "I'm just an idiot, but hey at least we know now!" He sat up clutching his chest "Although I'd rather avoid doing that again if possible, hurts like hell". Anne hugged him and then slapped him.

"Idiot" she said standing up but there was a smile of relief on her face.

"No more acts of bravado please, just follow my lead" Steve said and waved his hand for us all to get behind him, we did as he said and he stepped out into the corridor, stepping over the alien he had just shot he carefully picked up the gun and passed it behind him "Give this to whoever doesn't have a gun" he said and we passed it along the line until May who had been bringing up the rear took it.

"I really don't like guns" she said holding it in her finger and thumb.

"Let's just hope you don't need it" said Steve and moved on further down what looked like an endless hallway of metal and weird cables all over the place. When we finally reached the end of the corridor we came to another door.

"Let's do this properly this time" Steve whispered, looking at Alex who nodded back. Steve pushed the button and leapt forward, gun held high, the room was empty, it contained a few rows of benches and what looked like lockers.

"I guess this is where they change when they return from their little space trips" said May joining us in the room. I opened one of the locker doors and sure enough they contained the uniforms we had seen the aliens wear so far.

"Shame they look like dolphins or we could dress up as them" I said.

"Yeah, bit obvious we have human heads really" said Alex.

"Let's move on" said Steve and he approached the door opposite the one we had come in, pressing the button he saw no danger so stepped forward. It was at this point that everything went red and a very loud alarm began sounding.

"Oh crap" said Alex.

"We must have tripped an alarm" said Steve "Everyone run before they get here!" with that he ran down the corridor in front of him, his gun held out ready at all times. The rest of us followed blindly having no idea if something was about to come around the corner at us. The corridor opened out into a wider space with various tables and chairs, computer consoles and several exits, there appeared to be no one here, Steve rushed over to a bank of computers and knelt down.

"Everyone get down" he whispered, we all joined him, there was just enough room for us all to fit behind the consoles making us hidden from anyone coming out of the far doors, the door we had come through was behind us so we knew nothing should come from that direction.

"Keep very still and very quiet" Steve whispered, we all nodded in reply. I peeked through a small gap between the consoles and saw the doors sliding open across the hall, three dolphin people burst into the room, guns held high they looked around the room, seeing nothing they made their way to the door we had come from. This meant they were going to go right past us and the chances of being spotted were high so as soon as they came into view Steve leapt out firing. He managed to take down two of them before they even turned to see him, Alex followed shooting wildly and managed to hit the third in his shoulder, knocking him to the floor. Steve ran over to him, kicked the gun out of his hand and aimed his own gun at the dolphin like head.

"Don't move!" He said "Do you speak English?"

"Pathetic humans, we speak every language!" The X-Borg spat, but he didn't attempt to move.

"That's good, you're going to take us to your control room" Steve spoke calmly.

"You cannot defeat us, we are many, you are an inferior race..", Steve smacked the alien with the butt of his gun stopping him talking.

"Just shut up and get up, slowly" Steve said, the alien did as he was told and Steve spun him around and held the gun to the back of his head. "Now walk", as he said this the doors flew open and a dozen or more X-Borgs flooded the room, all of them armed.

"Get down!" Steve yelled and Anne, May, Beth and myself just had time to duck back behind the consoles before the bullets started to fly. Alex covered his head with his arm and was hit several times before he got down with us.

"Damn that stings!" He said, the suit protecting him from any serious damage.

Steve was using the alien he had caught as a shield, its body taking the bulk of the damage but a bullet made it through and struck him in the leg, clasping on to the alien he dragged himself towards us.

Anne began shooting wildly and randomly from cover, I saw what she was doing and did the same, soon the others joined in, the bullets flew about the room, occasionally one found a target but the majority of time the gunfire was just enough to deter the X-Borgs from closing in on us, then Anne's gun clicked empty.

"I'm out!" She shouted, the rest of us continued firing knowing we would all run out of bullets soon. I stopped shooting and crawled over to Alex who was breathing hard through the shots he had taken to the suit.

"This is hopeless" I said "We need help"

"What....aah.... do you suggest?" He replied in pain.

"Still got that doll?" I said.

"Eh? I think we need more than a good luck charm" He replied.

"Just get it out" I said, he gave a me look that suggested he thought I had gone mad but he pulled the doll out of his pocket, I took from his hands and held it up in front of my face,

"OK little guy, we are in a bind here and if you are going to do anything now would be a really great time" the doll remained lifeless in my hands "Come on you bastard! What's the point in me being the chosen one if I'm dead!" I screamed at the doll shaking it, nothing. "Dammit!" I threw the doll down on the ground.

"Dude, it's just a doll" Alex said patting my shoulder.

"I'm out of ammo" yelled May "Whatever you guys are doing you better hurry up!"

"We're screwed" I sighed defeated.

"Um...Jack?" Alex said tapping me on the arm.

"What?" I replied not turning.

"Look!" He said, I turned around to see the little doll stood up walking over to us "What the hell!"

"Yes!" I said "I knew it, please help us".

"I will help, I cannot lose the chosen one" the doll spoke.

"Holy crap it speaks too!" Alex gasped, the others were too busy shooting to see what was happening.

"Thank you, I'm ready, do what you have to do" I said.

"I think you have misunderstood" the doll said "You're not the chosen one, he is" it pointed at Alex.

"Me?" Alex said "Chosen for what?"

"Greatness" said the doll and he waved his little arm in front of him, as he did a blue light emanated from his hand and washed over Alex,

"Dude! What's he doing?" He asked me.

"Gifting you! I think anyway" I replied, I risked sneaking a peak at the enemy and fired a couple of shots towards them missing wildly. There were even more of them now and hardly any had been taken down by our amateur shooting.

"Anything happening?" I called back to Alex.

"Uh...yeah...you could say that" he replied, I turned to look and saw that Alex's hair and hands were on fire.

"Oh shit!" I said rushing to try and put the fires out.

"No mate, it's not burning me, it feels...powerful...it feels good!" He said and stood up.

"What are you doing!" Anne shouted "You'll be killed!"

"Don't worry. I got this" with that Alex walked out to face the enemy, they all turned to fire on him but the bullets seemed to not even reach his body before falling to the floor. Alex lifted up his hands and pointed the palms at the aliens, huge sprays of fire came shooting out of his hands, engulfing the X-Borgs in flames, they screamed and rolled around on the floor trying to extinguish the fire. It was no good, the fire was immensely hot and almost instantly flash fried the whole group of them, I cheered and applauded.

"Yes!! Go Alex" I yelled, the others stood up behind me to see what had happened.

"What the hell is going on?" Steve asked, dragging his wounded leg behind him.

"I'm a god-damn super-hero!" Alex replied, the biggest grin on his face, as he spoke the fire on his head and hands retreated leaving him looking normal and completely unscathed, the jumper suit must have been fireproof as well as bulletproof as it didn't have a single singe mark on it.

"Seriously?" Said Anne "Alex gets superpowers?" she rolled her eyes.

"I don't understand all this but he saved us so I don't care" said May.

"Well bugger me. This is certainly more exciting than being a bodyguard!" Said Steve smiling. I walked over to the doll which was now lying limp on the floor, I picked it up and held it in my hand.

"Thank you" I said, however somehow I knew that whatever had possessed the doll had left this body having completed its mission. I tucked it into my pocket nevertheless.

"Is anyone else hurt?" Steve asked, miraculously no one else had taken any injuries, the consoles we had shielded behind were riddled with bullet holes and would not have protected us for much longer

I walked over to Alex and slapped him on the back "Welcome to the world of abilities" I said.

"Pfft, mine are at least useful. You can be my sidekick though" He laughed and I laughed with him.

"This is very touching but we are not out of the woods yet, we don't know how many more of these things we will face before reaching the control room" Steve slid to the floor clutching his leg "And I'm not going to be much use to you, go on ahead without me".

"No way" Said Anne "We leave no one behind" she motioned over to me and we lifted Steve of the floor and put an arm each around our necks. Steve protested but not too much, we headed for the door the aliens had come from, stepping over countless still smoking bodies.

"Jeez that stinks" said Beth holding her nose.

"Crispy dolphin anyone?" Alex asked as he led the way across the corpses and out of the room.

46

Our trip through the rest of the ship was fairly uneventful, I guess most of the guards had responded to the alarm which was still blaring away, the lights bathing everywhere we went in red. We came across the odd X-Borg but it was clear these ones were not fighters and they surrendered peacefully when we aimed guns at them or Alex showed them his flaming hands which it seems he could now turn on and off at will.

Now armed with less hostile hostages we used them to lead us to the control room, Alex led the way, the rest of us using the hostages as shields as we entered the room. Several aliens were in the room and they turned shocked to see us but gave no resistance as we made them all sit in one corner of the room. Anne and I sat Steve down in one of the chairs and I asked one of the hostages if they had any medical supplies, he nodded and pointed to a unit on the wall. Alex ordered him to get the supplies and tend to Steve's injury, warning him of a fiery death if there was any funny business. The X-Borg did as instructed and armed with the medical kit he examined Steve's leg, he said the bullet had gone straight through and he administered a strange looking bandage to the leg. Upon contact the bandage took on the same colour and tone of human skin, Steve declared the pain had gone and stood up with only the slightest limp still evident.

"Now. Can someone turn that damn alarm off!" May said looking around the room, one of the aliens put his hand up and Alex motioned to him to continue, he went over to one of the control panels, flipped a switch and the noise and red lights mercifully stopped.

"That's better" said May sitting down in one of the chairs, her gun still aimed at the aliens in the corner. I had no idea who among us still had ammo and the hostages we had taken had not been carrying weapons to steal, but the threat of our guns, and Alex's new found skill, was enough to keep the enemy in line.

I ordered the X-Borgs to turn off the communication blocker, immediately as he did I could hear Calvin's voice in my head.

"Jack? Is that you my friend?"

"Good to hear your voice Calvin" I replied and went on to explain the situation, when I had done Tarquin spoke to me.

"Jack, you have done well, sorry I was wrong about you being the chosen one" He said.

"It all worked out for the best" I said and nodded at Alex.

"It sounds like it, I'm truly impressed you have got this far. Well done to you all"

"Thanks, but it's not over yet. We still need to install the virus but I already used it on earth." I said.

"No matter, with you being on the mother ship it will be a simple matter for me to override their systems and send them back to their planet". He replied.

"Are we not going to blow the ship up?" Alex said.

"Alex!" Said Anne "There could be women and children on this ship"

"This species is entirely male, they reproduce by cloning themselves so there are never any children but there are plenty of non-military personal on that ship and my race will not harm anyone if we can possibly avoid it". Tarquin explained.

"Fair enough" said Alex "Sorry guys didn't mean to scare you" he said looking at the hostages who were clearly terrified.

"Jack if you attach your communicator to the main console in that control room I can remotely program it from here to return to their own planet." Tarquin said.

"OK, but first I need to ask them a few questions" I said.

"Understood. Let me know when you are ready, time is no longer of the essence now you have commandeered the ship."

I turned to the aliens "I have some questions for you, who is in charge?" I asked, one of the X-Borgs tentatively raised his hand.

"I am the captain of this vessel" he said.

"OK. Is there any way to block that door from being accessed from outside?" I motioned to the door we had come in from.

"Yes, I can put the room in lockdown" the alien replied.

"Good, do it" I said, keeping the gun pointed at him, he stood up and went over to the main console, typing in a few commands a second door slammed down cover the first, it looked pretty impregnable. "Okay, now come away from there and sit down" I pointed at one of the chairs, he dutifully obeyed and I took a chair opposite him.

"I have a number of questions for you." I started.

"I want to know why they have dolphin heads" said Anne.

"What's a dolphin?" The X-Borg captain asked.

"Never mind" I sighed "We can discuss why alien races that speaks fluent English have never heard of dolphins later." I shook my head.

"What I want to know is, why me?" I looked intently at the captain.

"You mean, you don't know?" The captain asked looking shocked.

"No, I have no idea. I guess that you do" I said "So explain".

The alien shuffled in his seat, "Well, it's because....we made you".

47

The X-Borg captain explained that back many years ago my mother, who was a teenager at the time, was abducted and taken to this very mother ship. She was experimented on and returned back to earth at the exact moment she was taken; only now she was pregnant.

Her memory had been wiped so she had no idea any of this had happened, she was dating my father at the time so although they had been careful becoming pregnant was not a huge surprise. Apparently the aliens were attempting to create hybrid versions of themselves, in particular they were trying to breed female X-Borgs, I was the result of those experiments and although I turned out nothing as expected I had developed these abilities of mine.

It seems I have been abducted and studied many times over my life, each time my memory was wiped upon my return home, I was always returned at the same time I was taken so no one was any the wiser that I had even left.

So my mother and father knew nothing of this, as far as they were concerned I was a normal baby until the incident with my foot in my mouth, even after that there was no reason to suspect alien intervention. After all, I was a perfectly normal human being, I just had a power unlike any other, it seems the facility where I was studied had no idea aliens had become involved with humanity and no tests revealed anything other than a human boy.

The captain went on to say that the experiment, as far as they were concerned, was a failure, they had failed to mix the two species and also failed to breed a female X-Borg (he didn't call themselves X-Borgs but I can't pronounce their real name so for now we will stick with Alex's idea).

The experiment was abandoned and the species moved onto different things, ultimately this is where they decided our planet would be the next target for annihilation.

It turns out the X-Borgs feel their only reason for existing is to wipe out any species they consider 'beneath them', Earth, having yielded such poor results, was an obvious target. We were far behind them evolution wise and they felt as a species we would never amount to anything. I asked them why they felt the need to destroy everything and the captain looked at me like I was an idiot, his reply was simply "it's what we do" as if this explained everything. I moved on from that line of questioning as it seemed pointless to try and change the mindset of an entire species; instead I wanted to know more about how they could abduct people from different times.

He explained they had developed a machine aeons ago which allowed them to take any living being from any point in space or time and bring them to any of their mother ships that were nearby (by nearby he meant relative to their space capabilities which far exceeded our planets meagre efforts at space travel). I asked him if they were behind all the stories of alien abductions you hear around the world, he actually laughed and said those stories were all bullshit and that they took and returned people with no one, not even the abductee, aware anything had occurred.

Alex questioned if this meant they had a time machine, the captain explained that they cannot themselves time travel as we understand it, they could view the past using the machine and they could select certain matter and pluck it from its time zone and into their present. They could also contact people in the past but it was very hit and miss and the recipient had to be receptive to being contacted, even then it would appear unreal to them and often dismissed or ignored. He explained that this is what some humans believe to be ghosts, rather than the spirits of the dead attempting to contact the living it was actually his advanced race of alien beings using their machine. Anyone who believed they had seen or heard a ghost had actually been in the vicinity when the X-Borgs were investigating the past.

I asked if that meant they could talk to people in the past, he said they could but it was very rare that anyone understood what they were trying to say as the time difference and the difference in species interfered with any communication. They had little reason to use the machine for this purpose so it was not something they had ever cared to explore further.

Next I questioned him on why the others had been taken, motioning to Anne, May, Beth and Steve. He said that each person had been chosen because of their experience with me. It seems to finalise their experiments on the failed test they wanted to check people who had had a significant interaction with me, Steve and May had spent a lot of time with me throughout my developing years, Anne had, to put it bluntly, had sex with me and they wanted to test her to see if this had altered her DNA (they assured me it hadn't). Beth asked why she had been chosen as she had spent very little time with me, apparently her abduction was an accident, that occasion when she shook my hand and I let it go somehow tagged her as worthy of further investigation. It turned out her interaction had not been of significance in the experiment after she had arrived here.

I queried how I and everyone else could remember Anne's disappearance, he said it was due to the fact that they had yet returned to the correct time, once that had happened no one would remember them ever leaving. Steve yelled that they had no right to mess with time like that and the captain shrank away from him, it was clear this alien may have been a leader but he was no fighter.

Exhausted with all this information I slumped back in my seat to think, it was at this point that Beth came over to talk to the alien captain.

48

"So this means you can put people back to their correct time and space?" Beth asked.

"It does, and we always have done previously but when we were informed our experiment was interfering with our earth base we decided to keep hold of you all." The captain said.

"I want to go back" Beth said "Back to my own time, I have kids who will be all grown up now and will think I just up and disappeared one day" there were tears in her eyes.

"Can you do that?" I asked the alien.

"Of course, we can return you all to your correct place in history if that is what you require." He replied "But you must understand the process will erase your memory, you will have no knowledge that any of this happened.

I turned to the others "So who wants to go back in time?" I asked.

"Well I definitely do, in fact erasing all this would be a bonus" Beth said.

"I think I would like to go back too, I'd rather live my life as it was meant to be, not start again in my future. I assume everyone I know thinks I have gone" May said.

"She's right. All our friends and family will have moved on, if we don't go back it would be a hell of a job explaining where we have been over the years." Said Steve.

I turned to Anne and held her hands, "What about you?" I asked.

"I'd only go back if you came with me" She said.

"That is not possible I'm afraid. Jack was never taken out of time so the Jack of that era is still there. Sending him back would mean there would be two of him existing in the same space and time, which would cause catastrophic results to your universe." The captain said.

"Just how catastrophic?" I asked

"Well, you'd all be dead for one thing" He started

"Fine that's enough. What does this mean for Anne then?"

"Well she can be sent back to when we took her but that would erase your entire timeline, none of what you have done for the past seven years would have happened. Your human brain would not be able to cope with the influx of new memories and you would surely be rendered insane at best." He explained.

"Well that doesn't sound great either. But it's your choice Anne, I won't ruin your life" I looked her in the eyes.

"Jack, you could never ruin my life. I'm staying here, with you. I like the idea of you being my sugar daddy" She laughed nervously but it was good to hear.

"Are you sure?" I asked "It means losing seven years of your life"

"Meh, what are a few years between friends. I'm staying" she hugged me tight.

"Thank you" I whispered in her ear, when we ended our embrace I turned back to the captain.

"Do you understand what we want you to do? Send May, Beth and Steve back to their own time and nothing else." I said sternly.

"I understand, we can do that, as long as you release us" He said, I nodded then turned away from him.

"Tarquin, did you hear all that?" I said aloud.

"I did. I can work with that, once they have sent the others back I can administer the virus through your communicator, they will be sent back to their own planet and it will give us centuries before they can return." Tarquin explained.

"What about us?" Asked Alex "Anne, Jack and me? We don't want to be stuck on this ship forever!"

"We've got you covered. Once everything is set in motion I can activate a portal to your location, I will meet you at the entrance and guide you back to earth." Tarquin said.

"Looking forward to seeing you again, and meeting Anne" Isabella said.

"Me too" I said "Then it's decided, captain where is this time machine of yours?"

"It's in the science lab, twenty three floors down from here" He replied.

"Can you get us there without being attacked?" Steve asked.

"Yes, the lockdown I put in place will stop anyone from being able to traverse the ship without my authorization" He said.

"Just remember, anything funny and its crispy dolphin time" Alex said flames bursting from his hands.

The captain shrunk back in his seat "I still don't get what this dolphin thing is but your message is clear. You will have safe passage".

Alex turned to the other hostages who were still gathered in the corner, his hands were still flaming "Do any of you know what a dolphin is?" He asked, the group shook their heads and all replied in the negative. "Well that's just weird; I thought you guys had studied our planet".

"We have, but we have never heard of these dolphins you speak of" one of the alien crew spoke up.

"What about whales? Sharks?" Alex asked.

"Oh yes, we are familiar with all earthly marine life" the alien responded.

"Apparently not" mumbled Alex turning back to me "Okay, let's do this!"

I ordered the captain to stand up and lead the way out of the room, Steve, May and Beth followed, all of them had their guns at the ready.

"What about this lot?" Alex asked pointing to the crew.

"Good point" said Steve "We can't leave them in here with access to all the controls".

"Captain, do you have a secure room we can lock them in? One without any computers in it?" I asked.

"Yes, yes, we can put them in the officers' quarters, there are no controls in there and I can override the lock so it cannot be opened from the inside" he replied.

"Okay, good, everyone up!" I said "Alex you bring up the rear, any stragglers and you know what to do" he smiled and nodded showing his flaming hands to the crew as they marched past him. They cowered away from him and I knew they would not be any trouble, they clearly had not expected humans to possess such powers.

With the captain in the lead and me behind him with my gun pointed at the back of his head we made our way down the corridor, shortly he stopped and pointed at the door.

"These are the quarters" He said.

"OK, Steve, you mind checking them out?" I said, he nodded and entered the room, gun held at the ready, he swept the room like a true professional then called back to us.

"All clear" he said "Nothing in here they can use to stop us"

"OK, everyone but the captain inside" I yelled, they all obeyed without question, once they were all inside I looked at the captain "Lock it down" he waved his hand over the control panel which went from green to red.

"They cannot leave until I release the door" he said.

"That better be true" Steve said.

"We'll have to believe him, besides if he's lying he'll be the first one we take down" I smirked at Steve, making sure the captain couldn't see it. "Off we go" I said and our group continued down the hallway until we came to a large door.

"This will take us down to the science labs" the captain said.

"Okay, everyone in" I said, the others piled into the elevator as I Alex stood guard outside, once we were all on he stepping in after us.

"There's no buttons" He said.

"We don't need them, it all operates through a neural link in my hand" The captain began to explain, I stopped him from continuing.

"Never mind, just take us to the time machine." I waved the gun at him, he scanned his hand over a blank panel and we felt the elevator begin to move. Within a second it came to a stop.

"We're here" the alien said.

"I thought you said it was twenty three floors down?" said May.

"It is. Sorry it took a little longer than usual, will have to get that looked at" he waved his hand over the panel again and the doors opened, we all stood with our guns raised but there was no one waiting on the other side. We had come out on a metal walkway with various doors leading off of it.

"The machine is through that door" the captain said pointing ahead of him.

"Will it be occupied?" I asked.

"Only by scientists, please don't shoot them!" he pleaded.

"We're not going to shoot anyone unless they try something" Steve said "and you're going to be in front so if they shoot first you will be the one hit".

The captain visibly gulped, his dolphin throat bulging, we walked forward towards the door and waving his hand again the doors slid open to reveal the science lab and the time machine.

49

The room we were in was huge and totally dominated by a flashing, beeping machine that must have been the size of a three bed semi. Standing next to it were two dolphin men clad in the familiar white coats we all associate with scientists, it must be some kind of weird thing that all doctors and scientists must wear white lab coats, no matter what universe or planet they are from.

As we entered the two scientists were already on their knees with hands in the air, apparently the alarms and the subsequent lockdown had put them into survival mode. I walked the captain towards them.

"Tell them what we want" I said.

"Gentlemen, I will need you to fire up the machine and return these people to the moment in time we took them." He explained, the scientists nodded and immediately began preparing the machine. "It will take a short while to prepare" he said to me.

"Okay, you go over there and assist them, that way we can watch you all" I said, waving the gun in the direction of the other men. He went over and stood with the other aliens whilst they tinkered away. I found a chair and sat down, Alex came over and joined me, the others kept their guns trained on the X-Borgs whilst Steve watched the door.

"You okay mate?" Alex asked me.

"I guess, it's a lot to take in" I replied.

"Yeah. So...this means your dad is..."

I interrupted him "It means he's not my biological father, he's still my dad and always will be"

"Yeah of course. Still, bit of a whammy hey?" He said trying to lighten the mood.

"We have had quite the adventure this time haven't we?" I said "What about you? How are you holding up with what you've learnt?"

"What do you mean?" he looked confused.

"Well, all your life you've been looking for ghosts, now you find out they aren't real" I chuckled.

"Are you kidding? I've developed super powers and not only discovered aliens exist but my best mate is half X-Borg! It certainly trumps visiting haunted houses. And hey, you got Anne back, that's gotta make it worth it!" He said.

"It does. Despite all of this, I've got her back, someone I thought was lost to me forever" I smiled "oh and we saved the planet from being obliterated"

"Yeah that's also in the plus column I guess" Alex laughed and lightly punched my shoulder.

"One thing worries me though" I said.

"Is it the dolphin thing?" Alex asked, I laughed.

"No, no I'm just concerned that we won't know if they are telling us the truth, they could send the others anywhere and we would never know"

"Yeah good point, like into the middle of nowhere, or into the sun or something.....hang on I've got an idea" Alex pulled out his phone and began tapping away on it.

"Don't tell me that still works out here?" I asked.

"Yep. Don't ask me how but somehow I got signal once we arrived on this ship, 5g as well. I've been texting Lexa keeping her up to date on what's been going on" He replied, still looking at his phone.

"That's.....well that's not the weirdest thing to happen today" I said.

"Here we go" he showed me his phone, on it was a Myspace page for Beth.

"Whoa, old school" I said.

"Yep, but all the rage in 2006 when Beth went missing, it seems she was quite the active poster back in the day, until this lot took her and the posts just stopped." He explained.

"I get it, so we send her back and if the posts start up again we know she is in the right place!" I said.

"Exactly. And if she posts something like 'I was abducted by aliens' we'll know something went wrong." Alex was pleased with himself.

"That could work, if the posts don't start or they say something unusual we can force them to bring her back" I said.

"You got it. If they do this one right and they know we can prove it they will do Emma and Steve right too" Alex said.

"May" I said

"May what?" Alex asked, confused.

"No I mean her name is May, not Emma!" I said pointing at May.

"Then who the hell is Emma?" Alex asked.

"There is no Emma in this situation, you just made up a name like you always do" I punched his shoulder, harder than he had done to me but still in jest.

"Oh. Well whatever. If Beth gets back okay then we can assume Steve and...May will too".

I looked over to aliens, they were all stood waiting so I stood up and walked over to them.

"Is it ready?" I asked.

"It is" one of the scientist guys said.

"So you are aware, this device" I pointed at the phone Alex was holding "will prove you have carried out our commands correctly, so no funny business or it's bye bye aliens".

The X-Borgs looked at each other and then back at me, the captain was the one who responded.

"We understand. We have programmed the machine exactly as you specified." He said.

"Good" I said and turned to Beth "Are you ready to go first?" I asked her.

"Yes. I want to get back to my children and my life and forget all of this ever happened" She replied stepping forward.

"You will need to step into this machine and it will do everything you ask, I will now program it to your specific timeline" one of the scientist aliens said, wearing the same outfits and both looking like dolphins made it hard to tell them apart but it didn't really matter.

Beth nodded and handed her gun to Steve "I don't want to suddenly appear holding this!" she said, Steve smiled and took the gun from her. She stepped into the machine, it looked like one of those old tubes that offices would send inter-office mail to, only much bigger of course. So big in fact that Beth looked tiny stood inside the glass tube, I wondered if they used it for species that were significantly larger than us.

Turning around to face us Beth spoke "Bye guys, I'd say it's been fun but it's been the most terrifying time of my life" she attempted a smile.

"Good luck with everything" said Anne.

The door to the glass tube sleekly slid shut, encasing Beth inside it's core.

"This isn't going to hurt is it?" She asked, starting to look worried.

"I assure you, you won't even know it's happened" one of the science guys said, with that he typed a few commands into a console, I could see he was using the same symbol like script and we could only hope he was doing it right. He flipped a lever and the glass tube slowly turned opaque, as if it were misting up from the inside, within a few seconds Beth had disappeared from view. Another lever was flicked, a small flash of white light illuminated the tube then it went dark again, the mist dispelled and we were left watching an empty clear tube.

"It is done" said the captain.

"Alex?" I said, he started tapping on his phone again "Anything?"

"One second....here it is...yes!" he leaped a little in the air "She has posted many things, boring events like her kids birthdays and what not. Nothing about aliens or a trip into outer space".

"Well done, looks like you did it right" I said to the aliens.

"Of course. We are nothing if not honourable" the captain replied.

"Hmm, honourable but also planet destroying monsters" May said, the captain looked genuinely hurt at this comment.

"Who's going next?" I asked Steve and May.

"You go May, I'll keep watch until you have gone" Steve said.

"I'm not going to argue" May said and stepped into the tube "Bye all!"

"Bye May" said Steve and Anne together.

"I'll see you next week at my lesson...or not...I don't really know how this works" I said.

"It will all work itself out" the captain assured us.

"It better!" Said Steve forcefully.

"See ya Em....May!" Alex said, waving.

The machine went through the same process as it had with Beth and soon the tube was empty, once again Alex checked social media and once again it had updated to reflect she had never left. Following this we said our goodbyes to Steve and repeated the process with him, after he had vanished it was just me, Alex and Anne left holding the fort

"We have done as you asked, can we go now?" One of the scientists asked.

"Not yet" said Alex "There's one more thing we have to try".

50

Alex took me to one side and quietly spoke.

"There's been something nagging at the back of my brain and I finally realized what it is" he started, then went on to explain what he intended to do, Anne and I listened intently

"Okay, that does sound important" I said when he had finished "Let's talk to the scientists. Do you remember the exact date?"

"Strangely yes, it's like part of it was wiped from my memory but it must have always been there subconsciously" he replied. We went over to the alien science guys and told them what we wanted them to do for us, the reluctantly agreed.

"You understand it won't be like having a normal discussion? You will appear, at best, as ghostly figures" he said.

"We understand, we know what we are doing" Alex said.

"For once" I added under my breath.

"I'm glad you two know what you are talking about, I'll keep watch out here" Anne said.

The X-Borg tapped in more commands into the main console and led us to a different machine.

"This one will allow you to do what you ask" he said opening the glass door to a small cube like room with 3 glass chairs sat in the centre. I stepped in and took one of the chairs, Alex sat down in one of the others.

"Now no funny business while we are gone okay?" Alex said, small flames arising from the palms of his hands.

"Remember, I have all the guns!" Anne said.

"Understood. You will be perfectly safe" the captain said.

"Good, good, as long as we have an understanding" Alex said "Proceed".

One of the dolphin aliens flipped some switches and turned some dials, it occurred to me this could be some kind of vaporizing booth and we were about to be wiped out of existence, this thought occurred too late as the doors to the booth slid shut locking us inside. Besides, why would they have a boot setup to vaporize people when they had an army? I closed my eyes and the room started to fill with a blue tinged mist, 'oh great' I thought, it's a poison booth! But the mist did not appear to be causing us any discomfort and when I opened my eyes I was stood inside an old ruined building.

"It worked!" Said Alex "This is the place, remember?" Alex looked like himself except for one thing, he was translucent, I could clearly see him but I could also clearly see right through him.

"Yeah I remember. Can you see through me?" I asked.

"Yep, woooooo, we are ghosts!" He laughed.

"Let's go haunt ourselves!" I said and we tried to walk up the stairs but it was like walking on air and we didn't seem to move anywhere.

"Huh" I said "This makes it awkward"

"Here, let me try something" Alex said and began to concentrate, nothing happened for a moment and I thought we had messed up somehow but then Alex started to lift off the floor, only a couple of inches but he was clearly floating.

"See?" He said "Ghosts!" and with that he began to float across the room "This is great, try it!" I copied what he had done and concentrated on floating, sure enough I began to rise slightly above the floor, soon I was floating around the room with Alex.

"Great isn't it?!" He said "I'm going to try something else" with that he floated towards a wall and disappeared straight through it, a second later he appeared again coming out of the wall laughing.

"So we have full on ghost powers in here!" I said and copied what he had done, after a few minutes of messing around we heard voices and stopped still.

"It's them, or us, or whatever" I said, Alex nodded and we floated upwards, through the ceiling and into the room above.

"This is where it happened" said Alex "I can't believe I forgot" we waited for a moment and then a solid, younger version of Alex walked into the room looking around with a torch. He came towards us and walked straight through me, he shivered slightly but otherwise showed no sign of realizing we were there.

"Whoa, that was a weird feeling" I said "What happens next?"

"I have to get my own attention, give me the doll" Alex said, I pulled the creepy doll from my pocket and handed it to him, he floated towards himself, he put his hands on his past self's face and stared into his eyes.

"ALEX!" he shouted into his own face, the younger Alex froze in place, eyes wide open, mouth agape.

"Listen and listen carefully dude" ghost Alex said "You won't remember this but deep down you will know what to do. In the future you will visit a....weird shop....when you are there you must purchase this doll" he waved the doll in his old self's face "Do you understand?" The other Alex appeared to be in some kind of daze but he nodded all the same.

"You have to take it" I said.

"You are the chosen one" Alex said "Believe it or not!" he laughed and let go of his other face, at that point past me walked into the room and talked to Alex who snapped out of his fugue state, seemingly unaware of what had happened.

"Will it work?" I said as we floated back to where we first arrived.

"It worked before, we just didn't know about it" Alex replied.

"I thought it was weird when you wanted to buy that doll" I said.

"Meh, at the time I just thought it was cool looking, now I know I sowed the seed in my own mind from the future" Alex explained.

"Of course, we should have thought of that" I laughed and Alex laughed back.

"Ready to go home?" He asked, I nodded and standing at the same spot we had entered at we closed our eyes.

When I opened my eyes again the blue mist was receding and I could see we were back in the glass booth, the doors slid open and we walked out, Anne was still holding the guns on the aliens.

"Are you satisfied now?" The captain asked.

"We are." I replied "Now we need to return to your control room".

The alien sighed "Very well, come with me", we locked the science guys in the lab and the four of us returned through the elevator and down the corridor back to the main control room.

The room was empty, assumedly the others were still locked in their quarters, I sat the captain down in a chair and asked Alex to watch him as I went over to the main panel.

"Tarquin?" I said aloud "Are you there?" a few moments passed and I began to worry, then a familiar voice came over the communicator.

"Jack my friend! Calvin here, Tarquin will be joining us soon, he is just... umm...utilizing the litter tray" Calvin said.

"He's having a crap" laughed Alex.

"Well, yes indeed" Calvin said awkwardly "Are you well my friends?"

"We are, so far the plan is going well, now we just need to upload the virus and get the hell out of here" I said.

"I'm here" said Tarquin, slightly out of breath "You say you are ready?"

"Yep, just tell me what to do" I said.

"Okay, it's very simple, just detach the communicator from yourself and stick it to the side of the main console. Once that is done I can remotely set the virus running, I will have to talk to Alex with the next steps." He explained.

"Got it. Signing off for now" I said and peeled the communication device from behind my neck, I stuck it to the main control console and it instantly took on the appearance of it's surroundings. "You can tell him it's in place" I said to Alex he relayed the message to Tarquin.

"He says it's working" Alex said after a few moments, I nodded and looked around, various lights had started flashing and something was definitely happening.

"It's done" said Alex.

"What have you done to my ship!" cried the captain.

"Something you can't undo, but don't worry, you are quite safe, you will just be returned to your own planet" Alex was saying what Tarquin was telling him.

"My people will be most displeased with my failure" the captain said.

"Not our problem" I said.

"Tarquin wants to know if we are ready to come home?" Alex asked.

"Hell yeah!" I said.

"Good to go little kitty" Alex said, as he did a doorway appeared from nowhere, it floated in the middle of the room and slowly opened up filling the room with white light. Out of the light stepped Tarquin, Alex ran over to him and picked him up.

"Tarquin! My little ginger furball!" He said swinging him around the room.

"Nice to see you too Alex but please put me down, this is humiliating" Alex smiled and set the cat back on the floor he turned to me "Good job Jack, and this must be Anne, a pleasure to meet you my dear" he said rubbing around Anne's legs.

"Oh my god" said Anne.

"I'm sorry. I know a talking mutant cat is a bit of a shock" Tarquin said embarrassed.

"It's not that, you're just so cute!" She let out a little squeal and started to stroke Tarquin.

"I like this one Jack!" he purred "Ready to leave?"

"Yes please!" I said.

"Very well, Anne, if you would be so kind as to pick me up and hold Jack's hand, they know the rest." Tarquin said, with no hesitation Anne scooped him up and grabbed my hand

"See you dolphin dude!" Alex said taking my other hand; we all stepped into the portal together, finally leaving the aliens behind.

51

It was a Friday afternoon and Alex called me up on his way home from work.

"Mate, I just got paid and I've got a long weekend off work, wanna go out?" As well as his computer work Alex had a part time job in a video game store which meant he usually had to work over the weekend. It was rare for him to get Saturday off let alone the Sunday as well.

"Yeah I guess so" I replied half-heartedly, I was bored but the thought of socializing didn't fill me with glee.

"It'll be a laugh, I promise" Alex assured me.

"As long as it's not too busy" I said.

"Nah, we can just got to the Duck if you like, there will hardly anyone there on a Friday night"

"True. Okay, what time?" I felt a little better knowing we were just going somewhere I knew.

"Meet you there at seven?"

"So eight o'clock then?" I laughed.

"No way mate, I'll be on time tonight"

"Where have I heard that before? Fine I'll be there at seven, don't leave me hanging this time!"

"Would I?!" He said over-dramatically.

"Yes, yes you would" I ended the call and finished up the job I was working on, then got distracted watching funny videos on YouTube, next thing I knew it was six o'clock. I jumped in the shower and then threw some clothes on thinking I really need to do some washing.

51

I casually walked to the pub knowing Alex was unlikely to be on time but my mentality stopped me from being late to anything. I arrived at ten to seven so decided to wander around for ten minutes before going in.

Walking around the outside of the pub I heard a cat's meow, then muffled voices, was someone talking to a cat? I shrugged it off and checked the time on my phone, six fifty nine, perfect. I entered the pub through the rear doors and looked around.

To no surprise Alex was nowhere to be seen, luckily we were in here enough the staff all knew me so it wasn't too awkward going up to the bar alone and ordering myself a pint. The pub was practically empty so I picked a booth to sit down in and pulled up my phone.

I'm here I text, to my surprise it pinged straight back.

almost there was Alex's reply followed quickly by *sorry*

I sighed and sipped my drink, I was halfway through it when the doors flew open and Alex strode in.

"Ta Da!" he said "Made it!"

"Yeah, half an hour late, not bad for you!" I knew he would be late so getting annoyed was pointless.

Alex got a pint and joined me in the booth.

"So what's new with you?" he asked.

"Nothing much, the usual, working, sleeping" I shrugged "You?"

"Been looking through the paranormal forums again, think I may have found us a new place to visit, supposed to be super haunted"

"You've said that before"

"Yeah but this time I'm sure of it"

"You've said that before as well, so where is it?"

"Before I tell you, shall we get some shots in?" he was already standing up.

"I guess so, let's not get too out of it though" famous last words as the more shots we had the more we laughed and the more we drank, pretty soon I could barely stand when Alex suggested we go outside for a vape. We staggered to the rear doors and outside I slumped down in one of the plastic chairs, it was wet but I didn't care, I swore I could still hear the sound of a meowing cat but looking around I couldn't see one.

"You hear that?" I asked Alex who was puffing on rhubarb and custard vape juice, he stopped still and listened.

"Nope" he said and drew another puff "Come on, let's get another round in."

I didn't really need anything more to drink but it didn't take much to twist my arm, the pub was fuller now and we had to squeeze past a few people to get to the bar. As we stood waiting to be served Alex recognized some people who were also waiting, he introduced us and I drunkenly shook various hands despite having no idea what was going on.

The rest of the evening is a complete blank, I've no idea if we stayed at the Duck and Goose until closing or moved on to another pub, I also have no idea how I got home, the next thing I remember is waking up in bed with a missing hand, and that, my friend, is where you came in.

52

We went through the now familiar white light and came to another door, I pushed it open and stepped outside.

"Um, this isn't the pub, Tarquin?" I said.

"Oh dear, this isn't right!" The cat said, I don't know what happened next as I felt a smack to the back of my head and lost consciousness.

When I awoke we were in some kind of large building, another warehouse I assumed, my whole body felt constricted, looking down I could see I was strapped to a pillar. My jumper suit was gone and I was left in only my shorts, there were straps around my chest, waist, legs and arms, my captors were clearly taking no chances on me escaping using my abilities.

I looked around the room and saw Tarquin was inside a small cage, much like the one we had first used on him but with considerably stronger bars, he appeared to still be unconscious.

"You awake mate?" I heard Alex's voice from behind me.

"Yep, where are you?" I said craning my neck but unable to look far enough to see him.

"I'm tied up floating inside a bloody pool of water!" He said "They must know about my flame powers, sneaky bastards! I can flame my head but that's not really helping anything."

"Where's Anne?" I asked worried.

"I'm not sure where she is, she never arrived through the portal with us, I'm sorry boys, it seems we underestimated the enemy and they have managed to interrupt the portal to make it open elsewhere." Tarquin said shaking his head.

"What about the virus? Did it not work?" Alex asked.

"Oh that worked fine, I believe our captors are the X-Borgs left on earth, the planet is safe. We, I fear, are not" He explained.

"How come we are tied up, why not just kill us?" I asked.

"Because we want you to suffer" came a voice from behind me.

"Uh oh, dolphin dude!" Alex said, sure enough an X-Borg walked into the room and stood in front of me. This guy was huge, way bigger than all the other aliens we had seen, he towered over me and was built like the proverbial shit house.

"I know your powers now and I have devised these prisons to keep you captive, I will make you pay for sabotaging our plans and leaving me stranded on this pathetic planet" he said, an evil grin on his dolphin like mouth,

"Hah!" Said Alex "You're just pissed because we beat you!".

"You may have stopped our plans but the three of you are going to pay for it" with that he punched me in the gut, I screamed at the sudden pain, my body unable to curl up due to all the restraints. This guy had done his homework, I had no access to any of my limbs, even my fingers were tied together.

"Leave him alone you dick!" Alex yelled.

"Your turn will come human, first I want to play with this one" he pointed at me, I didn't think his idea of play would be in any way fun for me. From the pocket of his uniform he pulled a serrated knife, it was small but looked incredibly sharp, he began to run the flat side of the knife over my cheek.

"What have you done with Anne?" I screamed.

"I have no idea who that is" he sneered before quickly flicking the knife, I felt a sharp pain then warm blood running down my cheek, I winced in pain and clenched my eyes shut. The giant X-Borg laughed, "That's just the start of it, I know you can detach your limbs, I wonder what happens if I cut them off instead?" He sliced the knife swiftly across my arm, my eyes shot open and could see blood pouring from the wound but he didn't stop there, with quick movements the knife was slashed across my limbs leaving me bleeding from both legs and arms. My brain began to get fuzzy and I felt on the verge of passing out.

"You won't get away with this" Tarquin calmly said causing the alien to turn around; he walked over the cage on the floor.

"No one knows you are here and there is no one around to hear your screams, you have chosen a poor form to adopt. Maybe I should cut you open and find out what you are made of?" He waved the knife in front of Tarquin's cage.

"Hey Tarquin!" Alex yelled "Maybe you *should* show him what you're made of" I could practically hear the wink in Alex's words and realized what he was up to.

"Yeah, this guy has nothing on you Tarquin, let it all out" I managed to say through my dazed state.

"What are you two blathering about? I know this species is not built for fighting, this pathetic creature can do nothing to me" the alien said laughing.

"Oh I don't know" said Tarquin "I don't think you're ready for me, what do you think boys? Ready?"

"Oh yeah mate he's ready" Alex said, I merely gurgled my response and squeezed my eyes shut, just before I did I could see the confused X-Borg bent over looking at Tarquin, then light flooded the room. It stung my eyes even with them tightly shut, the only noise I could hear was the sound of the alien screaming in pain, after a few moments I couldn't take it any more and it was my turn to scream.

"Tarquin stop, please!" I screamed with the last of my strength, the light began to dim providing a blessed release from pain, I kept my eyes shut tight.

"Is it over?" Alex asked "Did it work?"

"It's done" said Tarquin "You can open your eyes", slowly I lifted one eyelid and sensing the danger had passed I opened my eyes wider, what I saw was the X-Borg lying on the floor, blood appeared to be running from his ears and eyes, he was curled up and shivering in a ball.

"Nice one Tarq!" Alex said "In your face dolphin!"

"He's still alive" I said.

"He won't be getting up anytime soon, besides he's blind and deaf at the very least, well done Alex for getting me to show him my true form" Tarquin said, he was returned to his usual six legged ginger cat persona.

"I figured it was worth a shot" said Alex.

"It certainly stopped him but we still have the issue of being trapped here"

Tarquin replied.

"Guys, I'm in a bad way here" I mumbled, drifting in and out of consciousness, I was losing a lot of blood.

"Shit! Tarquin, we need to get him to a hospital, can you get out of that cage" Alex said.

"I'm sorry, I don't have any more strength then a regular cat; there is no way I can get out of here." Tarquin sadly said.

"Jack, if you can still hear me you have to try something, my powers are useless in this damn tank" Alex said desperately.

"What do you suggest?" I said dejectedly

"Remember what Tallulah said.." Alex started.

"Tabitha" Tarquin corrected.

"Whatever, the doctor lady said you could control much more than just your hands, she said your power could let you do anything with your body" Alex pleaded.

"I don't know how!" I yelled "Every part of me is strapped down"

"Your head isn't" Tarquin said, it took me a moment to realize what he was saying.

"I can't detach my head!" I said

"Yes you can mate, you can do anything!" Alex shouted from behind me.

I screamed, then closed my eyes once again and began to concentrate, a strange sensation began to overcome me, suddenly all the pain went away and I felt like I was floating, and then my disembodied head landed on the floor with a thump.

"Oh shit!" Said Alex "Jack? Jack!" I opened my eyes and was presented with the sight of my own headless body hanging on a pillar bleeding out. Two things occurred to me; I had to do something or my body would die, and also, this floor is filthy.

I didn't think I would be able to speak but I tried anyway "It worked, I think" the words came out as normal.

"Thank fuck for that!" Alex said.

"Yeah but now what?" I said trying to see him but my view was blocked by my own body and the pillar.

"Remember that you can control your body parts even when they are not attached" Tarquin said.

"How does that help?" I asked, beginning to feel I was just going to die as a head lying on a dirty floor.

"Can you feel any pain?" He asked, once he said it I realized I couldn't feel the stinging from the cuts on my body any more.

"Actually no, I feel fine, but I'm still just a head" I replied.

"Try and move your body" he said.

"I don't see how that will help but I'll try" I fell into a state of concentration like I had learnt to do with my hand, watching my body I saw it begin to twitch, I managed to wiggle my toes, then my bound fingers. Soon I was able to control each and every part of my body, I even managed to suck my stomach in.

"So I can give myself a smaller belly, my body is still stuck" I said.

"Can you give yourself a bigger penis?" Alex laughed.

"Not now Alex, please" said Tarquin "Jack, you can feel no pain in your body, use that, use your powers to set your body free. You just detached your head without using your hands, that should work on all your body parts."

"I'll try" I said and began concentrating again, my body twitched and responded to my thoughts but for a while it seemed hopeless; I screamed and thrust all my thoughts into my body. Suddenly everything came apart; my feet and hands fell to the floor, my arms and legs separated at the joints which allowed them to slip out of the bindings, my torso, split in the middle causing both sides to slide to the floor.

"Oh crap" I said looking at the pile of body parts scattering the ground in front of me "now what?"

"Now you have to try and put your body together Jack" Tarquin said,

I looked at my hands, the fingers were still bound together but they could move as one, I used this to shuffle one of them around the floor. It was slow going but eventually I got the hand to the wrist it belonged to and lined it up as best I could, the lower arm seemed to move on its own and joined up with the hand.

"Yes!" I shouted.

"What's happening?" Alex asked.

"I'm doing what you are always telling me to do, I'm pulling myself together" I managed a laugh which came more from hysteria then humour, Alex groaned. I concentrated on the other hand and repeated the process until I had two arms with hands crawling around the floor. Once I got going it seemed to become easier, it was as if my body knew what it needed to do and was mending itself, I noticed as each body part rejoined its neighbour the wounds that had appeared seemed to instantly heal, leaving nothing more than a scar as if the injuries had occurred years ago.

Once I had my arms attached to my torso I used them as legs and 'walked' my upper body to my lower torso, once again they joined seamlessly, now I could drag my torso behind me as I crawled along the floor with my hands, the way they had been bound meant they were more like flippers, which made me laugh again as I thought of the dolphin species that had caused all this.

"Something amusing mate?" Alex asked.

"I'll tell you later, need to concentrate" I replied.

"It's working" said Tarquin, either to me or Alex.

Dragging my body along I reached the body of the twitching X-Borg and slid his knife away from him, it took some doing with my flipper like hands but I managed to grab the shaft of the knife between my thumb and bound fingers, now I just had to free my other fingers without lopping one of them off.

"That's kinda gross dude" Alex said who could now see my torso from his position

"Tell me about it!" I said, concentrating on the knife, finally I sliced through enough of the ties to allow my fingers to wriggle free; I used my free hand to take the knife and easily freed my other fingers. "That will make this easier" I walked my torso over to my head and laid down in front of it, bringing my hands up I rotated my head until it was lined up at the neck "God I hope this works!" I said, sure enough my body knew what to do and my head was at last back on my body.

"Fantastic Jack!" Tarquin said.

"Has he done it?" Alex asked, his view blocked again, I put my hands on the floor and 'walked' over so I could see him

"Ta da!" I said.

"Dude, that's just weird! But well done, now can you get me out of here?" His arms and legs were spread out and tied to the sides of what looked like a giant fish tank; his head was the only thing above water. His jumper suit had also been removed and he was wearing only his underwear, a pair of y-fronts decorated with images of Spongebob on them.

"Nice pants!" I chuckled "Let me get my legs on and I'll see what I can do" I hobbled over to the rest of my body and reattached my legs; it was a lot easier with working hands to fit my feet and leg parts together. I stood up and checked my body over, all the knife wounds had healed into scars which was good because dragging it along this floor I would surely have got an infection.

"It seems I have super healing as well" I said, walking over to where Alex was suspended.

"Very handy" he said, I took the aliens knife and slit the ropes holding Alex's arms in place, I passed the knife to him so he could do the same for his legs.

"That's better" he said climbing out of the tank and shaking water from himself, "bloody hell it's cold outside that tank" he shivered, I hadn't even realized but it was cold, freezing in fact and we were wearing only our pants.

"Warm us up and we can free Tarquin" I said to Alex.

"Oh yeah, almost forgot" with that his head and hands burst into flames, the heat warming us instantly. We went over and inspected the cage Tarquin was trapped in, it seemed to be made from solid steel with a large padlock holding the door shut.

"Damn, I thought this would be like a dog crate" I said trying to stretch the bars "you think he has the key on him?" I motioned to the X-Borg still twitching on the floor.

"I have a better idea" said Alex and he brought his hand close to the padlock "you might wanna move back Tarq" the flame on his hand shrank down until it was just one tight beam coming from his middle finger. Tarquin squeezed himself to the other side of the small cage as Alex used his flame like a blowtorch to easily slice through the steel padlock like it was butter, it fell off and he opened the door.

"You're free little dude!" He said smiling.

"How did you know how to do that?" I asked.

"Dunno, since gaining this power I just seem to know how to use it" He replied shrugging his shoulders.

"You both have my gratitude; shall we get out of here?" Tarquin said stepping out of the cage.

"Yeah, first I wouldn't mind finding some clothes" Alex said, we searched the warehouse and found our clothes lying in a pile inside a large container along with what looked like various alien machinery and weapons, the suits had clearly been sliced off.

"Well these are useless now" I said holding the tattered rags in my hands,

"Not at all, remember, these are not normal clothes, put them on as best you can" Tarquin said, I looked at Alex who just shrugged and draped the torn suit over him, I did the same. The clothes began to self-repair the rips and tears and moulded themselves to once again fit the two of us perfectly.

"I really am never wearing anything else" said Alex "These are so awesome".

"Glad you like them, I'll let Tabitha know you approve" Tarquin said.

"You might want to tell her to let people know they are bulletproof as well" I added "what do we do about all the rest of this stuff?" I asked, pointing at the alien tech inside the container.

"We can't leave it for others to discover" Tarquin said.

"And what about him?" Alex said pointing at the now still X-Borg.

"He's going to have to go as well; if he's found by humans it will open up a whole can of worms" Tarquin turned to face us "You boys up to this?"

"I guess we have to, come on Alex give me a hand" Alex and I cautiously approached the alien.

"Is it dead?" I asked. Alex tapped it with his foot; it did not stir so he kicked it harder, still nothing.

"I think so" he said "Grab his legs" Alex took hold of the alien's arms and I grabbed his legs, between us we dragged him over to the container and dumped him in with the other alien artefacts, it was hard work as he was a hefty beast.

"Well done, Alex if you would?" Tarquin said.

"My pleasure" said Alex and proceeded to blast fire into the container turning the whole thing into a huge fireball, the tech and the dead X-Borg melted together into one ball of mess.

"Someone will have fun trying to figure that lot out in the morning!" Alex said.

Tarquin nodded "Now we can get out of here and find Anne".

53

Exiting the warehouse we looked around the vicinity, it seemed we were back in the same district we had originally encountered the X-Borgs.

"Where do we go?" I asked.

"Calvin and Isabella drove back to the pub, we were supposed to appear through that portal" Tarquin said.

"Then we need transport, anyone have any money?" Alex asked. I rooted through my pockets, finding nothing but the now lifeless doll.

"I'm out" I said.

"Don't look at me, I don't even have pockets" said Tarquin.

"Can't you use your phone to pay for stuff Alex?" I asked.

"Yeah but I have no money on it" Alex said "Sorry guys"

"I can help with that, put your phone down in front of me" Alex did as Tarquin asked, he waved his paw over the screen and seemed to be doing something, after a few moments he pushed the phone back to Alex.

"There you go, I've put ten thousand English pounds in your account, is that enough?" He asked.

"Um yeah!" Alex was staring at his phone in disbelief. "How did you do that?"

"My body is still equipped to access certain technology, my entire race has the ability to manipulate electrical devices, including electronic banking, don't worry the money is completely untraceable." Tarquin replied.

"Dude! This is more money than I have ever had in my account, thank you!" Alex said stroking Tarquin's head.

"Well good. Now what's the quickest way back to your town?" Tarquin asked.

"Probably train, there's a station near here I think" I said, with that the three of us headed for the tube station. It was early morning and the city hadn't woken up yet but before long the early risers would be starting to appear.

"What do we do about Tarquin?" Asked Alex.

"What do you mean?" I replied.

"Well I don't fancy trying to explain a six legged cat on the tube to everyone we meet" Alex said.

"He's right, we need to disguise my abnormalities" Tarquin said.

"Hang on, I have an idea" Alex said and disappeared into an all-night Sainsbury's, he came back a few minutes later with a carrier bag.

"I had to buy some pop and snacks to get the bag" he said and handed me some items, putting the rest in his pocket he held the empty bag out to Tarquin "in you hop little buddy" he said.

"Really?" quizzed Tarquin "You couldn't find anything better?"

"Time is of the essence mate, we will have to make do, 50p that cost, not one of your cheapo bags" Alex replied.

Tarquin sighed and crawled into the orange plastic bag so only his head was peeking out.

"It'll have to do, come on" I said, Alex picked up the bag by the handles and carried Tarquin carefully so they didn't break. We made it to the tube station and sure enough Alex was able to use his phone to purchase tickets to Waterloo, the tube was fairly empty, just the odd shift worker on board and we arrived at the central station without incident.

Alex booked us two tickets for the next train back to our town; he gave me one and held on to the other.

"We got lucky, next train is in ten minutes" he said, we made our way to our station and boarded the train, finding seats furthest away from anyone else on board.

"Are your communicators still working?" I asked Alex and Tarquin.

"I'm afraid not, it seems the one who captured us was smart enough to remove them" Tarquin explained.

"Dammit, I need to contact the others and find out if Anne is with them" I said.

"I'll try calling them on my phone" Alex said pulling his phone out of his pocket, he held it to his ear for a few moments "straight to voicemail" he said.

"I hope they are okay" I said sitting back in my seat.

"I'll send him a text letting them know what we are doing, hopefully they will get the message" Alex tapped away on his phone, there was nothing to do now but wait until we arrived back home.

The train journey was uneventful, I think I dozed off a few times but was too worried about Anne to really relax, the trip only took about an hour and we were soon at our home town station. Stepping off the train we went over to the taxi rank, no cars were currently sat there so we waited, they usually turned up pretty quick but it was early morning so there were less about.

As we waited I spotted a vehicle in the distance heading towards us, Alex spotted it too.

"Is that?" he asked.

"It is!" I said "its Calvin's camper-van!" the van pulled up beside us and Isabella leaned out the driver's window.

"Hey boys! Need a lift!" She smiled, the rear door flew open and my heart skipped a beat as Anne came rushing out and threw herself into my arms.

"I thought I'd lost you" she said through her tears "I came through the portal and I was all alone"

"It's okay, we are all okay" I hugged her back hard; Calvin stepped out of the van.

"Greetings my friends, we found this one loitering around the Duck and Goose" he said, a huge smile on his face.

"They explained everything and looked after me" Anne said, finally pulling away but still clinging on to my hand.

"Thank you" I said "it's good to see you all again"

"The pleasure is mine, shall we depart this place?" Calvin said and motioned for us to enter the camper. We all piled in and Isabella drove us off.

"Where to?" she asked.

"I could do with a shit and a shower" Alex said.

"Have you still not pooed yet?" I asked.

"You know full well I can't crap in public bathrooms!"

"Ha, I know, just amazed you have held it in so long"

"Takes skills mate" he winked then to Tarquin he asked "Can you take me back to Lexa afterwards?"

"Of course, I will take you wherever you wish to go" Tarquin replied.

"I'd like to just go home please, I'm bloody knackered" I said.

"Righto, let's get you guys home!" Isabella said and off we went.

54

Later that day Anne and I were lying in bed; we'd showered, then made love, then showered again, Anne was tracing the scars on my body from where the alien had used his knife on me.

"You poor thing, so many scars" she whispered.

"Weird to think that they only happened yesterday" I said.

"I know, they look like they happened years ago"

"Don't chicks dig scars?" I laughed

"Well, I dig everything about you, scars and all" she ruffled my hair and planted a kiss on my forehead "come on, I suppose we ought to get dressed at some point today".

Anne leapt out of bed and looked around for her clothes, spotting her dress she held it up in front of her.

"Well I can't really wear this, it's filthy" she chucked the dress on the floor.

"Looks like you will have to spend the day naked" I grinned.

"Perv!" Anne laughed and rummaged through the chest of drawers before selecting an oversized t-shirt I had got free with a case of beer. She pulled it over her head and it hung low enough to be considered a dress.

"This will do for now" she declared looking down on herself, the shirt had a picture of a brown bear holding a large glass of beer, a speech bubble read "Cheers!".

"Looks better on you than it ever did on me. We'll go shopping later and get you your own stuff" I said getting out of bed and picked up her dress. I threw it in the washing machine "this will be clean for tomorrow"

"Thanks, I guess all my old clothes have long gone, it's like starting anew.

I suppose there was no one to miss me, I had no family after all."

"I missed you" I took her hand.

"Thanks, that means a lot" she looked around the small flat "so this is your bachelor den is it?" she smiled.

"It's not much, but it's home…yours too if you want it?" I sheepishly asked.

"Well I don't have a lot of choice at the moment so I guess it will do…for now" she gave me a cheeky smirk "it needs a woman's touch though"

"What's wrong with it?" I asked faking shock.

"Well the amount of socks lying around for one thing, not to mention all those video games and movie disks scattered around the room".

"I guess it could do with a tidy up" I smiled.

"Tomorrow" she said "Everything can wait until tomorrow" she pushed me back on to the bed and snuggled up close to me laying her her head on my chest, within a few minutes we were both sleeping peacefully.

We slept right through to the next morning, I made Anne breakfast of scrambled eggs how I remembered she used to like them, we were both starving so I had to make a second helping. Whilst we ate I ran Anne's dress through the dryer function on my washing machine so it was dry and warm for her to wear, it was really meant for basking in the sunshine, not the cold and wet weather of England but it would do for now. I suggested we go into town and pick out some new clothes for her; she was embarrassed that she had no money and I told her not to be silly, I would sort it out and besides I knew a cat that could help with funds. She gave me an odd look and I explained what Tarquin had done for Alex.

"Well in that case let's go shopping!" she said. We walked downstairs but before we entered my car I asked her to give me a minute and dashed into the shop below. Surprisingly someone new was on the till who I didn't recognize.

"Is Martin around?" I asked the new cashier.

"Day off today; said he had something he needed to do and asked me to look after the place" he replied not looking up from the magazine he was immersed in.

"OK, no worries" I attempted to peer beneath the counter, as far as I could tell the guy had normal human legs so I assumed he was probably not from

Martin's world. I left the shop and rejoined Anne.

"All good?" she asked, I nodded and pointed to my car.

"This is me" I said unlocking the doors.

"Mr. Fancy Pants" she laughed.

"It's a piece of crap but I own it" I shrugged.

"Hey as far as I remember neither of us could even drive so it's fancy to me" she kissed me before jumping in the passenger seat.

We drove into town and Anne picked out a few outfits as well as some underwear, I even got myself a couple of new t-shirts, we stopped at a café for a coffee and a sandwich, Anne declared that the town hadn't changed much in seven years, the only difference being more options of coffee than ever before.

After lunch we went back to my flat, Anne wanted to catch up on what she had missed in the last few years so she spent the afternoon glued to my laptop scouring Wikipedia. I tidied up the flat, even cleaning the bathroom and kitchen, when I was done she was still staring at the screen.

"Interesting stuff?" I asked nuzzling her neck.

"Yeah, just reading about covid, must have been a weird time" she replied not looking up.

"Yeah lockdown was.....different. To be honest I didn't really mind"

"Yeah you always did prefer social distancing" Anne laughing.

We spent the next two weeks returning to a semblance of a normal life, I had a lot of emails to respond to and work started to come in again. Anne managed to get a job working in the shop under the flat, no one seemed to know where Martin was but he had supposedly recommended Anne for the job. It meant I got staff discount on root beer so I was happy and Anne enjoyed being out of the flat for a few hours a day.

I hadn't seen Alex since the night we came back from space but he kept in touch with text messages and we agreed to meet at the usual place one Friday night.

"Come on, we need to get ready to meet the others tonight" Anne said as she stood up and kissed me. We had every intention of getting dressed but ended up making love once more, afterwards she insisted we really needed to get ready or we would be late. Reluctantly I got up and went to have a shave as I had grown quite the stubble over the past few days.

"No leave it" Anne said when she realized what I was doing "I like it" she stroked my cheek as I looked in the mirror.

"Yeah it is kinda cool, maybe I'll grow a massive bushy beard"

"Let's not go that far!" Anne laughed and skipped back to the bedroom to get dressed.

55

Anne and I walked to the Duck and Goose hand in hand, our shared experience bringing us even closer together than we were seven years ago, I might have been older now but Anne had always been more mature so it kind of balanced out.

We walked into the pub and looking around saw no sign of Alex.

"Typical, no matter how late we are he is always later" Anne said, we ordered our drinks and sat down in one of the booths.

"It feels weird being back here, knowing there is a portal to another world right through those doors" Anne pointed at the doors to the pub patio, as she did the doors swung open and Alex strode in, holding his hand was Lexa, she had only the one head this time.

"Jack! Anne!" Alex said as he came over and hugged us both.

"Good to see you mate" I said returning the hug "you too Lexa, I see you have lost a head".

"Tabitha managed to isolate the issue of human replication and so I asked to be normal looking so I could come to earth with Alex" she replied.

"I kinda liked the two heads but yeah it would have made it awkward" Alex said squeezing Lexa.

"I'm glad it worked out for you, for both of you" I said.

"I have you to thank Jack" Lexa said "it was your DNA that allowed us to perfect the process". She planted a kiss on my cheek and I actually felt myself blushing.

"Well glad something good came out of all this" I said.

"You also managed to save the entire planet" Isabella said walking in from the rear doors, Calvin was close behind.

We all hugged and said our hellos before sitting down, Alex bought a round of drinks for everyone which was a first. As we sat and caught up on what we had been doing the last two weeks more people came in from the patio doors, one was a short, ginger haired man I didn't know, the other I recognized as Martin from the shop.

"Hello all" said the ginger man, Alex stood up and put his arm on the man's shoulder.

"What do you think of Tarquin's new look?" he said.

"Oh my god! Tarquin?!" Anne said leaping up.

"It's me. I can now adopt this form whenever I need to visit earth" Tarquin replied, Anne hugged him and I stood up and joined in, turning to Martin I shook the man's hand.

"We were wondering where you had been" I said "I see you have legs now"

"Yep, no more tentacles for me! And since I no longer need to monitor you, my work here on Earth is done, but I wanted to come back and see you. Oh and to give you something" Martin said.

"It's not more fishy snacks is it?" I asked, Martin laughed.

"No, it's these" he handed Anne a pair of keys "I understand you have been doing a good job in my place"

"It's been fun, but I already have keys for the shop" Anne said confused.

"These are more symbolic, the shop is yours. If you want it?" Martin said.

"Mine? What do you mean?" Anne asked.

"I own the shop, the whole building in fact, and now you two do" he smiled.

"The whole building?" I said "Including my flat?"

"Of course, it's all yours the shop and the three flats attached, the deeds will be signed over into your names next week, you no longer have to pay rent" Martin replied.

"This...this is too much" I said.

"Nonsense, you deserve it" Martin clapped me on the back "And if you want you can change the shop to whatever you desire, or just sell the whole lot and go travelling, whatever you prefer"

"Thank you. Thank you so much" I said, Anne and I hugged him and we all sat down.

"This calls for shots!" Alex announced and went to the bar, he came back with a tray full of tequila shots, enough for two each.

We all downed the first shots then Calvin said one was enough for him, Lexa said it was revolting and Tarquin and Martin were not impressed.

"More for us!" Said Alex and we downed the second shots.

"What will you do now Lexa?" Anne asked

"I'm planning on staying here on Earth for now, with Alex" she replied grimacing as she sipped a glass of beer.

"We discussed staying on Lexa's planet but it was getting awkward with me being confined so as not to bump into anyone in their true form" Alex said.

"Besides, I kind of like Earth, this beer, not so much" she said but still continued drinking it.

"We'll find a drink you like, come to the bar with me" Alex said and they stood up to scan the shelves for different drinks, after trying a few she decided that rum and coke was her favourite. When he returned from the bar Alex asked me to come outside as he wanted to show me something, we went out to the pub patio area and he pulled out a shiny metal cubed object.

"Is that the metal from Tarquin's planet?" I asked looking it over.

"Check it out" Alex raised the box to his lips and a small tube rose out of it, he inhaled and exhaled a huge amount of vape smoke, it smelt of summertime, I don't know how else to describe it.

"Hooter made it for me, it's the ultimate vape mod, never runs out of battery, overheats or gives any dry hits." He took another puff and blew out a massive cloud.

"Impressive, what about the liquid? Where does that go?"

"A little funnel opens up at the bottom when you need to fill it and you just pour it in, he's working on a machine that allows you to program whatever flavours you want and it makes you the liquid."

"Like a coffee machine for vape juice?"

"Exactly!" Alex was clearly pleased with his new toy "He's going to let me have the machine once it's done" He took a few more puffs on the device before we headed back inside to join the others.

The evening was full of laughter and drinking, Alex and I doing two drinks for everyone else's one, we chatted about our adventures and general things, comparing life on our two different planets.

"So what will you do now?" Tarquin asked me.

"I dunno, hadn't really thought much past tonight" I shrugged my shoulders.

"We could use you and Alex in our investigations and you Anne of course" Calvin said.

"Oh yeah that would be cool!" Alex was excited at the idea.

"We have heard reports of a vampire in Portsmouth, couldn't hurt to have some powered friends along with us" Isabella smiled.

"I might skip this one if you don't mind, still trying to get my head around aliens and possessed dolls, your powers could be helpful against a vampire though Alex" I sipped my beer.

"Hells yeah! I'm game if you'll have me?" Alex was like a little kid wanting to go play.

"Of course my friend, a human flame thrower would be most useful against the legions of the night" Calvin did his booming laugh.

"Alright! Alex the vampire slayer!" Alex downed another shot of tequila.

"Then it is settled, Alex will join us on our next adventure!" Calvin raised his glass of Coke and Alex and Isabella did the same, clinking them together.

"What about you Tarquin?" I asked "What's next for you guys?"

"We have other planets and people to protect but as of yet we have no notifications of incoming dangers so for now I think I will explore your world for a little while, now that I can blend in with other tourists. You have many wonders on this planet that I would like to see, I've always enjoyed visiting other worlds. My people will call me in when the time comes" He replied.

"How about you Martin?" Anne asked.

"As much as I have enjoyed my time on this planet I would like to spend some time with my family back home before my next mission" Martin added.

"I never even thought about you guys having families" Anne said.

"Of course, the relationships of our species are reasonably comparable with your own" Tarquin said.

"I have a husband and three wonderful children" Martin said.

"You must have missed them dreadfully whilst here on earth" Anne said touching his hand.

"I still got to see them when the shop was closed but yes I would like to spend some quality time with them now my mission is complete"

"That's cool, so Tarquin, anyone special in your life?" Alex asked.

"He's always been a loner" laughed Martin.

"It's true, never really found time to settle down, maybe one day" Tarquin looked thoughtful; his thoughts were interrupted by the barman calling last orders.

Alex got one more round in before the evening came to a close. Tarquin and Martin were the first to leave, exiting through the back door and into the portal; promises were made to keep in touch.

Calvin and Isabella drove off in their camper-van as we waved from the pavement leaving the four of us to walk home. I was extremely drunk at this point, Anne was not much better and Lexa was slurring her words and giggling a lot. Only Alex who seemed to have the constitution of a horse was standing upright, the walk back was heavy going with us staggering to and fro, eventually we parted ways with Alex and Lexa and stumbled back to our flat.

"I can't believe we own all this" Anne swayed from side to side as she looked up at the building in front of us "I might have to make some changes".

"Whatever you want babe, can we do it another day though?" I slurred.

"Come on piss-head" she laughed.

"Hey you're just as pished" I managed to blurt out.

"I've got seven years of drinking to catch up on" she giggled.

"I don't think it works like that" the two of us stumbled upstairs where I threw my clothes off and collapsed on the bed.

I awoke the next morning and although the night before was a bit fuzzy and my head was, as usual, throbbing, everything felt right with the world.

As I lay there I realized that I had found my 'woods' again, it wasn't so much a place as a state of being. I felt serene with Anne sleeping peacefully

55

next to me; with her in my life again maybe things would finally be okay.

Somehow through all this craziness I had come through relatively unscathed, my useless powers had actually done some good, hell I'd helped save the world! Huh, maybe this *is* a superhero origin story after all?

I rolled over onto my side and lifted my left arm to stroke Anne's hair.

56

Goddammit!

About the Author

Oliver Trusler hails from the south of England but now lives in Yorkshire where he looks after other peoples cats at a local cattery.

So far none of them have had more than the standard four legs.

You can connect with me on:

https://twitter.com/oliver_trusler

https://www.facebook.com/profile.php?id=100090628714403

Printed in Great Britain
by Amazon